DANGEROUS FRIEND

by
Barbara Topley-Hough
and illustrated by Joanna Roberts

HENDERSON
PUBLISHING PLC

©1996 HENDERSON PUBLISHING PLC

Chapter 1
A Secret

"Sam! You're driving me crazy. Whatever's the matter?" asked Isabella, as she watched her cousin pacing the room.

" - er - nothing - er - well it's those girls. Just listen to that racket." Sam was looking a bit uncomfortable.

"You're lying!" Isabella said airily. The twelve year old pair had known each other all their lives. "But I know what you mean. Sophie and BeBe really know how to get your mum going," she laughed.

At that moment a voice rang through the house. "Hurry up you two! Get a move on! We're going to be late!" There was silence. "Sophie! BeBe!" It was Sam's mum. She sounded anxious.

" - oh, they'll be ages yet if I know them," put in Sam, always ready to stir. "Adding the finishing touches - a bit more eyeliner here, a touch of lipstick - oh that lipstick!" Sam pursed his lips in imitation as his mother appeared in the doorway. He liked to amuse Isabella and he usually succeeded.

She stifled a giggle as the two girls swept into the room. "Oh, not for an interview!" she said.

Both girls - Sophie, sixteen and BeBe, fifteen - wore jeans, tight, very tight. Sophie had a black silk scarf around her neck and a black sweater revealing her new Wonderbra; and earrings, long of course. Her hair stood up punk-like from last night's party and her lips bore traces of the purply-black lipstick she liked so much. Isabella thought she looked great. BeBe - well - BeBe's decor was a little less contrived. Her hair too was plastered down to the nape of her neck, party-style, and below she sported a long Black Hawks ice hockey shirt, a present from an old boyfriend who had passed through Hong Kong the previous Christmas. She had at least taken out the seven earrings from the top of her left ear.

Sam and Isabella were full of admiration. They weren't lacking in judgment though. They waited for the explosion. It came. "What do you think you've got on?" Their mother approached them like a bombshell. "You can't go for an interview looking like that. That hair! Both of you! You'll have to wash it."

The truth was, Sophie and BeBe didn't want to go to a boarding school. They didn't want to go into a strange sixth form. They didn't want to leave Hong Kong and all their friends.

Sam's mum pushed the pouting pair upstairs. "And the nail polish must come off!" Her voice could be heard from the landing amid the splash of running water.

"Come on Bizzie." Sam hit his cousin gently on the top of the head, feeling her silky black-brown curls. "It's going to rain tomorrow. This might be our last chance for a game."

"Okay. You get the racquets. They're in the boot of the car. I won't be a minute," said Isabella. "I must say goodbye to Sophs and BeeBs - and Aunty Charlotte. I might not see them tomorrow." She ran upstairs, kissed her cousins, pulling a face in collusion at their dripping hair.

"See you in Hong Kong. Roll on July!" she said.

"Be good!" said BeBe.

"And if you can't be good be careful!" added Sophie, which is what her father always said to her when she left for a party.

Isabella loved being part of the girls' set-up but as she and Sam were the same age - twelve, nearly thirteen - they were usually together, which wasn't bad either.

Sam had not always been better on the sporting front than Isabella, but in the last year he had grown. How he'd grown! He was now a good head taller than she was. Quite good-looking, Isabella thought on the quiet, especially the eyes, blue-blue with heavy lids. People never failed to comment on the cousins' darkly fringed, large blue eyes. Isabella often wondered if she was as striking. To look at she was so different, but she couldn't help knowing that she too was very pretty. People in the street often turned to look at her. Was that conceit to be aware of that? Of course not! It was her liquid half-Indian eyes, shapely expressive mouth and that tumbling mass of hair.

She tossed those curls, just like they did in the books she read, in defiance at Sam's speed on her dad's rusty old bicycle. By the time she got to the tennis court, Sam was already winding up the net. Isabella grabbed his racquet and helped him measure the height of the net. Soon all an observer would have noticed were two long-legged youngsters flying around the court; puffy white clouds overhead; the consoling, almost rhythmic ping of tennis ball on strings. It was a scene that belied the fierce panting battle between the pair.

"Bother!" screamed Isabella lunging on her backhand, her back to the net and Sam. She sprawled full length on the shale court. Sam ran to the net.

"Are you okay?" he asked.

There was silence for a moment. Then Isabella got up laughing and rubbing her right knee.

"Fat lot you care! Had you worried though didn't I? Crikey, how did you get that one back?" she panted, wiping herself down.

Sam looked momentarily sheepish. He'd won the first set six-three, and after that last shot he was leading five-two in this set. It hadn't been like this a year ago.

Into the eighth game Isabella won the first two points - thirty-love. "I'm not going on any longer," she shouted to Sam across the net, and at Sam's questioning face, she added, "You're just giving me points." Again Sam looked guilty. He had not been trying his hardest.

"Don't be silly, Bizz. At least let's finish the set."

And they did. It was a big defeat for Isabella.

"I can't believe how you've improved," she began. "Have you been having coaching? You were brill!"

"N-no! No!" Sam's face went through a series of emotions in such rapid succession that Isabella looked at him straight in the face.

"You have. I know you have!" she went on.

"Honest! Cross my heart and all that!" But Sam still looked a little strange and strained.

Isabella shivered involuntarily. Something - something she couldn't put her finger on was happening. What was it? How was it? Sam was different - somehow. Puzzled and worried - why was she worried, she wondered. Isabella searched around for something to say. It was un-usual for them to feel awkward with each other.

"Mum says I can come with you in the taxi to the airport to meet your mum and Sophs and BeeBs." She cleared her throat. "What time's the plane?"

"Two-thirty, I think," replied Sam.

"Lucky thing! I'd love to be going to Hong Kong with you tomorrow." Isabella looked wistful. But she was herself again.

"Well it's only six weeks - seven - eight - and you three will be coming out," said her cousin.

"Not Dad. He can only spare three weeks, but Mum'll be there. She wouldn't miss it for anything, like me," she laughed. "And then I'll beat you! Tennis club, here I come!"

"Shall I put your name down for the Junior Doubles?" Sam asked.

"Yes sure! Oh you mean playing with you? Will you condescend to have me as your partner after today's showing?"

"You weren't that bad!" Sam laughed.

"Only you were brill! But I might just find an even better bet! Your pal Danny looked pretty good to me!" Isabella squinted at her cousin from beneath her thick lashes.

"Pfhu! Danny! Well I can tell you - "

"No boasting!" Isabella intervened. "I'm not interested in the number of times you've thrashed the living daylights out of him."

It was time to change the subject. After all, they were good friends and today was their last day.

"Do you think the girls will get in?" she asked.

" - to the school? Not if they can help it! They really don't want to leave Hong Kong, but Dad thinks they'll stand a better chance of getting good grades if they go to school in England - and so they'll be more likely to get into university," said Sam.

"Is that what they want?" asked Isabella, wondering if that's what she would want to do.

"How should I know what they want to do! Sisters! Big sisters are a pain. I couldn't possibly claim that I could enter into their tiny minds and read their innermost thoughts. I can think of nothing I'd like to do less!" He paused. "Actually they are quite clever - or so their school reports say, although I've never seen any evidence of it myself!" Sam looked at Isabella to see how all this was going down. She was smiling at him in an indulgent grown-up kind of way.

Slapping her sturdy thighs she sprang up from her cross-legged position at the back of the court.

"Come on! I'm famished. Mum says we can have a burger and coke for supper. The gang's coming round for your last night - but they'll have to leave by ten. Your flight to Hong Kong and all that!"

☠

"I will! I will! I will!" Isabella called to her mother who was waving goodbye standing at the front door.

"Please don't be late at the British Museum. Chinese Section, Room 33," called her mother.

"I won't! I won't! I won't!" laughed Isabella.

The engine of the taxi was chugging away quietly. Sam was putting his suitcase in beside the driver's seat. He slammed the door.

"BeBe's! Crikey, hold on! BeBe's suitcase!" Sam called to his Aunt Sarah, who disappeared into the hall. Sam went to meet her as she struggled with a huge soft black case.

"I'm sorry," he said. "Why BeBe can't take her own rubbish, I don't know," he said irritably.

"Wouldn't go into the hired car. What has

she got in there, it weighs a ton?" Isabella's mum heaved it over to Sam.

"Just clothes," returned Sam. "Jam-packed with clothes - but mostly she wears clothes that fit six foot five rugby players, so they take up a lot of room. Sisters!"

"You wouldn't be without them!" laughed his Aunt Sarah. "Off you go now," she said as she slammed the door for a second time. "See you in July. Isabella - remember - by the brass Buddha Protector in the corner."

Isabella stuck out her tongue and opened her eyes to look as if they were popping out, showing her mother that she knew exactly what the Buddha Protector looked like.

Sam climbed into the taxi. Isabella had left a lot of room but he sat bang next to her.

"Shove up a bit!" said Isabella looking at the space on Sam's left. Sam looked over to his left... and moved a couple of inches.

"Sa-am!" Isabella peered over him.

"What on earth was that?"

It had been a brilliant flash of lightning followed a few seconds later by an ear-piercing roar of thunder. Suddenly the skies opened and huge drops of rain hit the windscreen. They had only just noticed how dark it had become. It seemed cosy inside the car and somehow exciting, too.

"Good thing we set off reasonably early," called the driver from the front. "It's going to be slow in this deluge."

10

"You'll miss the plane," grinned Isabella, "and then you'll have to come to school with me."

"Not likely!" retorted Sam. "They work you far too hard at your place. No early maths for me!"

"I wish you'd move up." Isabella gave Sam a push. "It's hot!"

Sam stayed where he was, resisting her.

"Bizzie - listen. I've got something to tell you," he said, looking at his cousin uncertainly.

"Fire away, I'm all ears. The floor's yours. Shoot."

Sam continued to look at her but was silent.

"Go on then!" Isabella was half laughing but also wondering what had got into Sam. "You're an oddball!" she added. "Whatever is it?"

"Promise - promise you'll never tell anyone - " He paused.

"Tell them what? So far I've got no info." Her smile broadened. "You haven't murdered someone, have you?"

"No - Bizz. This is serious. You have to promise," said Sam dropping his voice.

"Pro-o-mise," said Isabella flippantly.

"Not like that!" Sam was annoyed.

"All right." Isabella looked suitably serious. "I do promise, Sam. But tell me."

"No matter what hole you're in - no matter how difficult it is to keep my secret - promise you won't ever spill the beans." Sam was looking almost shifty.

"I said I promise. That should be good enough. I don't go in for that hokey-pokey-cross-my-heart-stuff." said Isabella pausing, "I promise!" she shouted loudly enough so that the driver turned round.

"What a day!" he called to the pair. "Does it rain like this in Hong Kong?"

"Worse," said Sam, flashing a look of impatience at his cousin. "Sometimes whole buildings slide down the hillside."

The driver cast a disbelieving look over his shoulder.

"Honest," Sam said. Then he surreptitiously moved the screen over slightly so that it made it more difficult for the driver to hear what the cousins were saying.

"Well then?" asked Isabella very quietly.

"And promise you won't laugh?" Sam half-grinned at her.

"Well you know me - that's a bit of a tall order - but I'll try not to," she said.

"I have a friend," said Sam looking ridiculously serious. There was silence for a moment.

"Well fabuloso! Bully for you!" began Isabella. "I always thought you had lots of friends!"

"No, not an ordinary friend - " he began.

"A girlfriend! Hee, hee!" cackled Isabella, rocking to and fro and holding her sides exaggeratedly.

"Shut up Bizzie. Now I won't - " Sam interrupted again.

"Go on, please. I do promise. I was just joking," said Isabella, now putting on a deeply serious face.

12

"It's not a joke," said Sam. "I have a special friend - a different kind of friend - "

Isabella's eyes grew rounder by the second but she kept her mouth firmly shut.

"An invisible friend." Sam sat back in his seat, glanced over to his right and drew quickly back to Isabella, searching her face for a reaction.

" - you mean like - like very small children have when they're very lonely - ?" She paused. "You mean you made him up?" Isabella went on. Her mouth was beginning to twitch at the corners. She mustn't laugh.

"I didn't make him up - he just arrived one day."

"Is he here now?" asked Isabella quietly, shivering slightly.

Sam nodded. He looked over to the empty space on the seat.

"So that's why you can't move up?" Isabella asked.

Sam nodded again.

For a few moments there was silence between them. A long jagged light cut through the air and again another shattering crack of thunder. The pair almost jumped out of their skin. The rain pelted the windscreen making it difficult to see out. The cousins were in a world of their own, but it didn't seem cosy any more and perhaps it was a shade too exciting. Sam looked a bit uncomfortable.

"Actually, he's very nice," he said.

"He's a boy, is he?" asked Isabella. "You mean he's just arrived? Where did he come from?"

"I'm not sure really - but definitely not from England," said Sam decisively.

"How can you be so sure?" asked Isabella agitatedly. "I mean, when did he arrive? And where were you when it happened?"

"I was in Hong Kong, at home. And it was years ago. I can't honestly remember. It seems as if he's always been around - "

"Then he was one of those - those playmates that lonely children - one of those imaginary friends. And somehow he's never gone away." Isabella felt quite annoyed without knowing why.

"You think I haven't grown up, don't you Bizz? Well you're wrong. I wish I hadn't told you now. I thought I could trust you to be understanding - " he said in a very grown-up way.

"I'm sorry, Sam. But this is such a shock and kind of creepy."

"No, it's not creepy. I've told you - Minx - "

"Minx!" burst in Isabella. "Minx is a girl's name. Like, 'oh you little Minx'. It's a girl!"

"No, it's not! And it's not an 'it'. Minx is - well - nice - he often helps me. You know - like when I'm playing tennis - "

"You what? So that's how you've got to be so good? Of all the cheats!" Isabella was really shouting now.

And Sam was beginning to feel sorry for himself. He'd never tried explaining Minx before, just taken him for granted. It wasn't easy.

14

"Bizzie, for goodness' sake calm down. Minx is a friend I've always had - for as long as I can remember. I can see him and no one else can, that's all - "

"That's not all," interrupted Isabella again. "I mean - what does he look like? How old is he?"

"He's no age really," said Sam as Isabella rolled her eyes to the heavens. "I don't know what age he is. I think of him as being about the same age as I am. And he's Chinese," he said in a rather satisfied kind of way.

"Isn't that rather confusing that you can see him and other people can't? I mean, do you find yourself talking to him - and people thinking you're bonkers?"

"No, I don't really talk to him - at least not often. We just - well - communicate!" Sam went on.

"I don't understand at all!" said Isabella, exasperation in her tone.

"Well, Minx - he's a kind of guardian angel - at least that's how I think of him - I don't think I ever found his presence confusing - he helps me like I said," sighed Sam, wondering if he was getting through at last.

There was silence for a moment. Isabella was thinking.

"So how come you suddenly decided - after years - to tell me about him?"

Sam looked as if he was wondering if he should tell his cousin more.

"It's because - just lately Minx is becoming -

well - too much for - he can be very naughty - a bit of a nuisance. I needed advice - and you're pretty good at telling people what to do - "

Isabella burst in once more "Oh thanks - "

"I didn't mean it like that," continued Sam in a conciliatory way. "You're wise - older than your years. Dad's always saying so - how grown-up you are and how childish I am."

"Sorry about that," laughed Isabella.

"Anyway Minx has become difficult, restless - and I've been bothered by this. And also I wanted to tell you because - in a way - you're my best friend, almost as good as a boy."

Isabella looked taken aback, but half flattered. She'd always thought of Sam as her cousin. But of course he was a friend, probably her closest friend too. However, she couldn't help continuing to think that Sam had made things up.

"Sam, do you think Minx came into your life because you wanted to be Chinese?" Isabella asked.

"How did you know that?"

"Don't know, but I've often thought you did - " she smiled.

"Yes, when I was younger I used to think how nice it was - that they all lived on top of one another. Sort of cosy, friendly. The kids all did their homework on the shop counter, all together in the evenings. They weren't banished to their own rooms. Maybe they all even slept together. I used to think they did - in one big bed. I don't imagine for a moment they do really," he laughed. "But I don't know why he came to me. He just did that's all."

"But you're telling me because I'm half English and half Indian. You think maybe I'd like to be something different - ?" Isabella asked.

"Well, would you?" Sam looked at her questioningly.

"Certainly not! I really like - well - being both - know more people - have more friends - different friends," she said.

"Yes, I can see that. I told you about Minx for the reasons I said. Minx is restless. Advice please."

"What do you think he's restless about? Does he want to leave you, do you think?" she asked.

"Maybe - I must admit I hadn't thought of that. It's hard to imagine being without Minx!" Sam looked positively alarmed.

"And what's all this about tennis?" asked Isabella.

Sam heaved a huge sigh.

"Mmm - Minx is good at all ball games and he always wants to join in - lately especially."

Isabella looked at her cousin very suspiciously.

"You mean he wins points for you?" she asked.

Sam fixed Isabella with a steely look and finally nodded.

"I can't stop him. I mean tennis is nothing - you should see some of his rugby tackles."

Isabella couldn't help smiling.

"At least that made me feel better in a way. I

reckon without Minx's help I'd knock the you-know-what out of you!"

"Could be!" agreed Sam with mock dejection. "Sometimes it's really embarrassing because I feel as if it's obvious that I couldn't have hit the ball or even got to it."

"I must say, once or twice, I thought I was seeing things - but then everything happened so quickly." Isabella was beginning to enjoy the revelation.

She looked past Sam to the empty space. "Couldn't you ask him to show himself to me?"

"Well, I could, but I don't think he'd take any notice. He doesn't like direct approaches, even from me," said Sam in explanation.

"Do you talk to him at all?" she asked.

"In a way - but not like I'm talking to you - I think things - okay, sometimes I say them out loud - and sometimes Minx replies. Mostly he doesn't but he is good at giving advice - sometimes when I don't even ask for it. He has been getting above himself lately."

"What's his reaction to me? Does he mind that I know?" asked Isabella.

"He hasn't commented," Sam replied. "Do you find that insulting?" he laughed.

Isabella ignored the comment.

"I'd find it - well - funny to have someone around all the time, watching my every move - but in some ways I can see it is quite nice to have a companion. Is he always there when you wake up?"

"I think he is, but I'm so used to him that I'm not really aware of his presence - I know he's there though - then suddenly when I need him, he gets more into focus," said Sam, now more relaxed.

Isabella tossed her mass of curls. "A bit of a cheek really! Here are you with two sisters - and me, an only child and you have a constant friend," she said resentfully.

"I am an only child," said Sam. "Sisters don't count - at least mine don't!"

"Do Sophie and BeBe suspect?" she asked.

"You what? Goodness no! Bizz if you - "

"Hold your horses! Of course I wouldn't. I've told you, I'll tell no one."

"Can you imagine them with info like that? My life wouldn't be worth living." Sam looked horrified.

"Look, the rain's stopped." Isabella rubbed the steamy windows.

"And we're nearly there."

Suddenly he felt his world and Isabella's drifting away. They both sighed involuntarily with relief.

Straight to the coffee shop on the first floor they hurried. Sam's mother and sisters were already there. Sophie and BeBe were looking glum - and hardly recognisable in their fresh blouses and skirts, faces well-scrubbed.

"They've got in," said Sam to Isabella out of the

corner of his mouth. "Just look at their faces!"

Isabella couldn't help a giggle. Her two glamorous cousins looked the picture of misery. There were kisses all round, the interviews had been a great success, but Sam's mum was looking at her watch.

"I'm afraid we'll have to go Bizzie-Bo. The plane leaves in an hour."

"You're sure you'll be okay?"

"Of course - it's only about forty five minutes on the train and then I'll be meeting Mum at the B.M.," said Isabella.

There were goodbye kisses and Isabella walked with the four to Immigration. They all waved and Sam took a last look back. Isabella was mouthing something. He screwed up his eyes trying to understand her stage whisper.

"What does he look like?" Isabella looked intently at him.

"What - what?" Sam ran back to the entrance.

"I said, what does he look like? You didn't say," she said.

"He's Chinese," said Sam hurriedly. "Quite big eyes," he added thinking aloud, "and a lot of hair - a heck of a lot of hair." He ran back to join the others.

Isabella nodded, temporarily satisfied, and set off to meet her mother at the British Museum.

The train journey passed in a flash. Her head buzzed with thoughts of Minx. At one station when a young Asian man with a mass of hair got on the train, she jumped out of her reverie.

20

In Room 33, she could see her mother talking and gesticulating to a group of people she was showing round the Oriental Room. Isabella looked over to the brass Buddha Protector in the corner where she was to meet up.

Why did they always have to look so rude, she thought and stuck her tongue out in return.

She wandered around. There were a lot of Oriental people there.

Suppose we're all more interested in ourselves than others, she thought as she surveyed the scene.

She came upon an even more horrific brass figure in a case. 'Twelfth Century Guardian King of the North. Wu Han.'

"Ugh!" she shuddered.

The King was standing on skulls. She counted nine pairs of hands, each holding more skulls. On his head were balanced heads which had not yet become skulls, but that could be their only fate; and over the back of his shoulders was a seemingly live captive with a terrified look on his face.

And these would be in temples, she thought. What danger is there in China that they need all this paraphernalia?

She moved to the stone Monkey God.

"He's very naughty!" Isabella almost jumped out of her skin at the sound of her mother's voice behind her. "That's why he has that cap on. The Goddess Kuan Yin tightens it whenever he steps out of line so that he gets a terrible headache. But he did help Tripitaka bring the Buddhist Scriptures from India to China. He's so mischievous though and gets above himself - like someone else I know." She laughed. "Did Sam and co. get off all right?"

"Fine," said Isabella.

She was rather quiet on the way home. She felt odd. Her bones were her bones and her skin was her skin. But were they? The real her? Her body was something she could look at from the outside. Surely all this Minx stuff was ridiculous. She'd let herself be carried along by Sam. He was just trying to impress her - trying to be one up. But what was Minx? Was Sam just imagining things like a small lonely boy? And if there was a Minx, who was he?

"A ghost?" Her lips pursed as she finished the dreaded word. Then if he is a ghost, he must have been alive one day. But what else? What else? Are there ghosts all around that we're too stupid to see? She shuddered. Who gets to see them? Did Minx choose Sam? And what about me? She pulled her knees up to her chin. Will I ever see him? When does a ghost stop haunting and move on? Sam didn't seem to feel haunted. She loosened her grip on her knees. Sam seemed happy enough. What about ghosts? Are some good and some bad? Minx didn't seem to be bad - only a bit naughty. She was mouthing each thought silently.

She sighed a deep sigh. She was curled up again into a tight ball. She was cold - so cold.

I'm not going to think about it any more, she told herself. But even as the car pulled into the driveway, back to the safety of home, her head was still buzzing with thoughts and questions about Sam's friend, Minx.

Chapter 2
Just a Face

It was one of those early summer days when every blade of grass sparkled. As Isabella cycled to school for the first day of the summer term, she felt the day was reassuringly like many other school days. Over the four miles between home and school the navy-blue blazers and their yellow badges became more numerous and now and then stretched dangerously four abreast across the road.

"Hi Bizzie!" called Poppy, a good mate of hers. "Wow you're moving. Wait!"

Isabella looked over her shoulder, wobbled, thinking how she'd hardly noticed that she was passing everyone. What was her hurry, she wondered.

"Great night!" said Poppy catching up.

"Did you think so? I hardly saw you. Weren't you deep in conversation with Sam?" Isabella laughed.

"Mmm," said Poppy enthusiastically. "Very dishy!"

"Dishy! My cousin - never - " which was not what she really thought. He was - she had to admit - dishy. She had known Sam all his life - and hers - so the warts were not entirely hidden.

"And so interesting," continued Poppy. "I mean he wasn't like most boys - he didn't mention cars or cricket - and he didn't boast once!"

"What was so fascinating then?" Isabella shuddered.

The wind blew through her hair. Surely Sam hadn't told Poppy as well. She was momentarily indignant.

"Reincarnation!" called Poppy who was now in front of Isabella. "Tell you in a mo."

I'll be annoyed if he has, thought Isabella. All that stuff about needing my advice - and being my best friend -

"Do you believe in reincarnation?" Both girls were now pushing their bikes side by side through the front school gates, as Poppy turned wide-eyed to her friend.

"Don't know much about it," replied Isabella. "What exactly is it anyway?"

"Well, it's not being dead when you're dead." Poppy shrieked and collapsed with laughter.

"Only you could think of an explanation like that," smiled Isabella. "Isn't it coming back - being born again after you're dead?"

"Something like that. And it's about getting better too. Being a nicer person second time around. Indians call it trying to reach Nirvana - perfection - nothingness. You should know all about that stuff."

"You mean about being a perfect person?" Isabella deliberately misunderstood.

"Ha! Ha! No, all about Indian religion."

"I do know a bit about it but not from my dad. Mum's into that sort of thing though - a bit of an intellectual, my mum. And did that take you the whole evening - that bit of sacred knowledge?"

"No. Sam was telling me about the Chinese gods that are sent back to earth because they misbehave in heaven - and how some gods are always between heaven and earth, helping people out." Poppy sighed. "I really like the idea. I mean, it's living for ever, isn't it?"

"But you might be a fly, or a crocodile."

" - a crocodile wouldn't be bad, basking in the sun all day - "

" - or a child in Ethiopia or some other place where they have a rotten time," Isabella went on.

Poppy looked thoughtful for a moment. "But I do believe in it, don't you?"

"Naah!" Isabella's lips curled. "Plain old heaven'll do me!"

"Some hopes you've got," Poppy laughed.

The school bell rang. The first day of term was always noisy and this was no exception. School had its good side - and its bad. All those endless talks about working for exams. Isabella's first lesson was computer studies. That was okay she thought - usually. She was good at that.

"I'll see you all individually this lesson," began Mr Jackson, "so just carry on from where you were last term. I'll be teaching nothing new for the moment." There were sighs of relief all round. "It's consolidation and practice for the exams."

There was an audible "Ugh!" from the back row.

Isabella took the hood from her computer

26

and stowed it away. She flipped through her manual and found the relevant page. Shifting in her chair ready for full concentration, she opened up her computer, waited, then moved the arrow to 'Isabella', and waited again. The screen was blank. She was about to move the arrow again when the X key moved on its own. She jumped. A small X appeared on the screen. The same key moved again and again. Faster and faster, it continued insistently.

"Sir! Sir!" Isabella put up her hand. But with the shuffling of papers, quiet click of the keys and the usual class whispering, he didn't hear Isabella's voice nor see her upstretched hand. Her computer continued to play the insistent X's; sometimes thick ones, then thin, now large, then small; sometimes spaced then crowded together until beneath a spray of the same heavy black X, two round staring eyes emerged. Isabella panicked. She looked to both sides. Poppy was peering intently through her thick-lensed reading glasses while George on her left was flipping through his manual. Isabella switched off her computer. The screen cleared and was once again a comforting dark grey.

She waited a moment, took a few deep breaths and braced herself defiantly. She wouldn't bother Mr Jackson just now. And again she opened up the computer. Moving the arrow to 'Isabella', she waited. She was watching that key now and she didn't have to wait long before it recommenced its self-appointed work. Slowly she raised her eyes to the screen. The black spray of haystack hair was still there, and below, those eyes - eyes that stared straight back into hers - eyes, which though round were tilted upwards at the corners - unmistakably Oriental eyes. The Xs, line by line, shaped and shaded that Chinese face like the police identikits shown on TV when they're searching for a man on the run - a murderer.

Isabella sat motionless, held by that face. Her lips then, silently formed the word, 'Minx'. Could it be Minx's face? Oh Sam! 'A heck of a lot of hair - big eyes.' That's what Sam had said. This has nothing to do with me, she thought. Tears of indignation and fear started to well in her eyes. Why did you have to bring me into this? All the expressions of those thoughts about her cousin spread across her face. She closed her computer down once more, pushed her chair back and picked up the manual. What did all this mean? And more to the point, what was she going to do about her computer? Mr Jackson was only three desks away from her. Could she delete the whole of two terms' work, Minx and all?

"You've had enough for one lesson, have you Isabella? Finished - shut down for the day?" Mr Jackson asked sarcastically.

"Oh no, Sir - just - just - consolidating like you said." Isabella flashed her most winning smile.

"Well get on. It's practice you need."

28

Isabella's heart sank as she opened her computer once more, moved the arrow to her name for a third time and waited. In full glory, that face was lit up again. The eyes returned her stare but now they seemed almost friendly, as if in communication. She glanced over her shoulder. Mr Jackson was talking quietly to the boy behind her. She raised her manual to shield the screen from prying eyes, hiding it from her own perplexed eyes as well.

"Now then Isabella. Where are you up to?" Mr Jackson took the manual from her.

She looked up at him as his gaze focused on the screen before her.

"That's good," he said shortly. "No problems it seems." He scanned her work quickly. "That's an interesting way round section five, but it seems to work."

Isabella turned her head sharply and faced the screen, breathing an enormous sigh of relief as she did so. No face. No Minx. All her two terms' work safely restored in all its amazing normality.

Quickly recovering herself she said, "I think I can carry on on my own, Sir."

The bell cut through the concentration of the class. Computers were closed down. Isabella shuffled, just like the others, out into the corridor. Poppy was chattering on, not noticing her friend's blank stare.

"I'm hungry." Isabella sprang back into life. "And I'm really looking forward to tennis practice. I'm determined to get into the team this term."

"You will," said Poppy, not in the least bit envious. "Too much like hard work for me. But I'll come and watch."

Down at the courts the friendly sound of the ping of tennis balls reverberated back and forth, shortly followed by occasional shrieks of dismay.

"Shot!" George, standing racquet in hand at the net, looked over his shoulder at Isabella. A sizzling backhanded ball had just whizzed past his left ear, completely shattering their opponents on the other side. Fifteen-love. Isabella again served hard but the ball bounced against the top of the net back to her side of the court. Her second, gentler serve got what it deserved, but once again with her back to the net, she delivered an unbeatable backhand. And so it continued. She and George crossed in the middle of the court.

"Come up to the net when you can, Bizz," he said quietly, smiling. "They just might get some of those drives back. You know we could make first couple at this rate."

Isabella did not return his smile and served again. Forty-love. And finally for the fourth point, she dashed to the net as George had advised and smashed the ball into the right hand corner of their opponents' baseline.

"I don't know how you got to some of those," said George admiringly as they left the courts for afternoon lessons.

"Nor do I!" began Isabella. Her voice was flat.

"Your backhand's transformed, but it'll pay us for you to come to the net when you can - even when they're serving. I've never seen you smash like that. And you seem taller. Have you grown?"

"Oh shut up! It was probably just a fluke."

"No, false modesty! That's not like you," George called over his shoulder as he entered the boys' changing room.

The look on Isabella's face was one of deep annoyance. Another of the tennis players slapped her on the back

"Gosh, you were brill, Bizz. Is that Sam's influence?"

What a cheek! She wasn't taking that. But maybe it was his influence. She had never played like that in her life and she knew she was being helped - helped like Sam had been. The whole of that last game had been out of her control. She liked being a success, but not like this. As she walked from the changing room to the science block, a quiet wind ruffled her hair against her cheek. She whipped round to look behind her. There was no one. Now she had two problems and the term was only just beginning. Where would the next one come from?

She wondered what she could do about the computer. She'd have to check it again. That would mean getting hold of - stealing - the key to the computer room. And then that Sam! She'd have to get hold of him somehow. She couldn't imagine Mum agreeing to a phone call when she'd only seen him the day before. In any case he'd hardly have arrived back in Hong Kong. Fax him. But what could she say on a fax knowing that Uncle Justin would be sure to see it first?

Afternoon school seemed endless. There was plenty of trouble for Isabella, trouble of a perfectly normal kind like tellings-off for getting her experiment all wrong; a danger to the class and all that. The bell rang at last for the end of the day.

"See you at the bike shed. Don't go without me, Bizz," said Poppy. "I've left my pencil case in the classroom."

"I've got to - I've got to meet Mum," said Isabella, hesitantly, "so I'll be going into town. I'll meet you at the church in the morning - half past eight. See you then."

"Okay, see you. I might need to ring you about the maths," Poppy called.

"Do that."

Isabella hung around the cloakroom until she was pushed out by a prefect. She walked determinedly along the corridor outside and up the main staircase. Along another well-lit corridor, she could hear voices coming from the staff room. She slipped into one of the classrooms and waited behind the door. Footsteps and voices gradually disappeared, until at last there was no one about, not even a cleaner. Stealthily she opened the staff room door. The room was empty and unusually tidy. She walked hurriedly across the room and entered the stock room. Many keys hung from many hooks. She'd never find the right one. Room 14. Room 15. Library. Secretary's Office. And then - at last, Computer Room.

She ran back through the staff room only remembering when she was halfway down the corridor that she'd left the door open. Back at full speed she went, her heart beating hard. Down the staircase she skipped meeting Miss Redfern at the bottom.

"You played well, Isabella. You've got a lot stronger," said their tennis coach.

"Oh thank-you Miss!" She didn't want compliments and especially not at this moment. She hurried on, her smile changing once more to a look of grim determination. She fumbled with the key in the lock, but she was soon inside.

"Now then you - you - Minx! I'm going to get rid of you once and for all!" she muttered between her teeth. "It's only a question of a page, a face. Just a face!"

She leant over her computer and in so doing her dark curls fell on to her cheek. It felt as if her cheek had been touched by someone. She shot round. Once more there was no one - not even Mr Jackson! The screen lit up and the arrow lighted on 'Isabella'. She had only to wait a moment and the dark face reappeared. It seemed to be mocking her. The face was full of life, fashioned in the same way as those police identikits, but more real, rounded, lifelike, ready to step out of the screen into the world.

"Get rid of it," she whispered. "Get rid of the page."

She pressed the word 'delete', but nothing happened. The face continued to look at her. Minx refused to go away.

"Damn!" she hunched her shoulders, exhaled, and half stamped her foot.

"I'll bin the whole lot!"

Tears began to roll down her cheeks.

"I don't care how much work goes down the drain."

Her hands were shaking as she moved the arrow to highlight the whole folder. She pressed 'delete'.

"I don't care!" She almost shouted.

But her efforts were in vain. She didn't have control over the computer. Minx did!

She put her head down on the keys and ran her fingers through her hair. She remained head bowed for several minutes, then she threw herself forcefully against the back of the chair.

"All right Minx. You win. But don't think you're my friend. You're Sam's friend, not mine."

She tapped her palm impatiently against her thigh. Then she got up, gave one last glare at that Chinese face and closed the computer down.

Back on her bicycle she had never cycled home so fast.

"And I don't want help with my tennis either!" she shouted at the top of her voice as she sped past the courts.

The fax machine was staring her in the face

as she opened the kitchen door.

"That you Bizzie?" her mother called from upstairs.

"Yes, only me, Mum." Isabella's voice sounded so tired.

What could she say to Sam if she did send him a fax? Five-fifteen. Then it's plus seven - or is Hong Kong eight hours in front at this time of year? It would be at least midnight. Sam's mum hated faxes clicking noisily through in the middle of the night. She'd do nothing. She'd wait - but Isabella wasn't very good at waiting or at doing nothing.

She was in bed by eight that night.

"That's the way to start the term, Bizz," said Dad as he kissed her goodnight.

Isabella hardly had time for one of her smart one-liners back before a wide yawn had taken her into a deep sleep.

The church clock struck. Isabella was wide awake and counting. It was midnight. The house was completely quiet. She started as the curtains billowed into the room. Surely she'd closed the window.

What's that? She knew it was the wind, but even so she threw back her duvet and approached the open window. The chill of the air gently wafting in made her shiver. Outside streaky grey clouds half hid a slivered moon but many stars sang out from the navy blue sky.

"And the highwayman came riding, riding - " She whispered the poem to herself.

Half laughing now, she noted that she had the right hair!

"Better a highwayman than that bloomin' old Minx!"

Again something - the curtain - brushed against her cheek. There was a clicking sound. Isabella stood stock still. Then slowly turning her back to the window, she looked around her bedroom. The teddies, her old dolls, her clown stared back at her. Everything was as it should be - except for the clicking. Opening the bedroom door, she stepped on to the landing. The door of the spare room was open and the curtains pulled back. Dad's computer was on, the screen was lit. That black haystack of hair was already in place and the eyes were beginning to give it meaning. She moved swiftly over and turned it off. The face seemed to resist, but in the end it had gone.

The rest of the night was fitful as she tossed and turned. She was tired in the morning but a totally uneventful day put her mind at rest. Computer studies was computer studies; and her tennis was back to its usual form. George was sad about those smashes. Then two more happy days elapsed and Isabella had almost totally forgotten about Sam and Minx.

Another sparkling day found her taking a short cut to the lich gate to meet Poppy through the churchyard. On the bumpy path before her she suddenly saw two round, fluffy objects. They were thrush fledglings. They can't fly - they must have been injured, she thought, standing her bicycle up against a gravestone. As she bent down to pick one up it fluttered for a few yards, just off the ground. It was then she realised that they weren't hurt, only learning to fly. Smiling, she picked the other one up.

"Come on. You'll be safer up here." And she perched it on top of an upright gravestone.

Determinedly she followed the other as it hopped away from her.

"There. There's nothing to be afraid of," stroking it and feeling its tiny heart, beating so fast, she whispered to the second one.

She placed it with the other one on the gravestone.

"Oh no!" she whispered. Before her on that same stone she read:

Isabella died...

When did Isabella die? She panicked, half putting her hand out to feel the letters and the blank space.

Afraid, she withdrew her hand, then started violently as a draught of air - a hand perhaps - the wind - touched her black curls. Turning swiftly she saw that a large thrush had swooped down on her and was now winging its way back to the branch of a tree from where she had been watching her young.

Isabella touched the back of her head and was still shaking when she heard a welcome and familiar voice.

"Bizzie! Come on, it's twenty to," called Poppy.

Isabella looked up. "Come and see," her voice was hoarse.

Poppy leant her bike on the gate and ran over.

"They're sweet," she said.

"The mother's just dive-bombed me - " began Isabella.

"Hey, look!" said Poppy. "Isabella died here in 1796. Creepy! Sorry!" she laughed.

"1796? Where does it say 1796?" Isabella peered carefully at the stone. She felt the outline of the numbers with her hand. "So it does!" She sighed with relief, continuing to stare at the faded numbers.

"You're a weirdo!" laughed Poppy again.

"Oh, do you think so?" asked Isabella seriously, sounding hurt.

"Of course not! Come on! We really are late now."

Isabella had a sinking feeling. Was it starting all over again, or was this just her imagination? But she couldn't afford to sink today because the tennis team was to be chosen. George was in high spirits, full of attack during the knock-up. Isabella was full of trepidation. Her backhand had completely gone to pieces.

"What's happened to you Bizz?" asked George as they collected the balls from the base line.

"Just wham it like you did the other day," he encouraged.

"All right I will!" Isabella gritted her teeth.

A few of her early shots were really wild but as the game progressed, she relaxed and was playing well. She couldn't put a foot wrong. They really were a strong pair and played so instinctively well together.

"Oh, shot Bizz!" called a friend from the sideline as Isabella produced the backhand of her life, the final shot.

"And I did it on my own," she muttered to herself between clenched teeth. "That'll show him!"

George and Isabella were chosen as first couple for the junior team and were all set for a good season.

"We made it!" she said triumphantly as she opened the back door of her home. Of course her mother knew immediately what she meant.

"Well done! Was it close?" her mum asked.

"Pretty, I think," said Isabella modestly. "Hannah and James played very well but it was just luck that it was our day."

"By the way, there's a very strange message for you from Sam on the E-Mail today."

"Oh?" Isabella's face clouded. She had not been expecting to hear from Sam. He was no great letter writer. And frankly she had not hoped for one.

"I did a print out. It's here. Total rubbish - or is it code? What's he being so secretive about? Is he in love?"

"Don't be silly, Mum. Anyway you shouldn't have read it."

Isabella took the print out and went to the privacy of her bedroom. Her hand was shaking as she unfolded the paper.

'JCXGP'V UGGP OKPZ UKPEG K IQV QP
VJG RNCPG. ECP AQW JGNR?

Love Sam.'

"Oh heavens!" she thought. "Whatever's all
this about?"

She used to use a code with Poppy for notes
in class.

'ABCDEFGHIJKLM
NOPQRSTUVWXYZ'

"How would that look?" she said to herself
as she began to decipher the message.

'EPCJ' she wrote. No, that doesn't mean
anything. But if I know Sam he could have
easily got his own code wrong! What does he
think I am? She sighed.

Then she tried -

'ABCDEFGHIJKLM
ZYXWVUTSRQPON'

"Okay. Let's see."

She wrote 'IKZ - '

"Oh yes, very fruitful!" she muttered with
deep sarcasm.

'KZAVP!'

"Yeah, yeah, yeah!"

She stomped downstairs.

"I can't make head or tail of this Mum. Do
you mind if I send a message back?"

"No, carry on. Can you do it?" her mother
asked.

"Not the opening bit, but the rest's all right."

Her mother set up the computer for her

E-mail message to Sam.

"Don't make it too rude!"

"He is the limit!" exclaimed Isabella.

"It must be a deadly secret, that's all I can say," laughed her mum.

Isabella typed -

'Dear Sam,

I can't make head or tail of this. Try again.

Love Bizzie.'

She looked at Sam's message again. Not another secret from Sam she hoped - or perhaps it was the same secret, a message about Minx. There were several four letter words. She couldn't make 'Minx' out of any of them. Perhaps Sam had taken to using rude words! She couldn't see any way to interpret the code into those words either. She gave up and sent off the E-mail message.

That night was warm, but even so she closed her window firmly. She fell asleep, her head a confusion of thoughts and feelings, pleasures and irritations. She was very pleased about her tennis form, but she had lurking fears about Sam's message and the return of Minx. The return of Minx. Of course she'd never seen him. The coward! Too scared to face her. Sleep and wonderful oblivion came at last.

She awoke feeling cold. It was beginning to get light. She looked at her watch. Three-thirty on a summer's morning. What was that? The same computer noise came from the spare room. She began to shake. The window! It was open and the curtains wafted gently in the soft wind.

She opened her bedroom door cautiously. From the landing she could see the lit computer screen. That Oriental face was slowly emerging once again. The quiet click of the X in its many forms gave a subtle shading below the slanting eyes down to a wide, full mouth and finally to the small square chin, ghostly in the early morning light. She wanted to hurry back to her bed but she was drawn on by those eyes - those eyes which she knew were blank and unchanging but which she, in spite of herself, imbued with life.

She took a deep breath. She'd tell Sam - get him to do something. She could send an E-mail right now. She knew what to do. She opened up the E-mail. It worked, and thankfully Minx was hidden from her. But there on the computer was another message from Sam. It was a horribly long message that was as complicated a code as before. She took out a piece of paper and a pencil from the drawer to copy it down; irritated, half excited, but certainly less afraid than she had been a few moments ago. She had a job to do and Isabella was good at jobs.

'OKPZ! JCXG AQW UGGP OKPZ?'

OKPZ again, she thought.

'OKPZ JCU IQPG. K TGRGCV JKU PCOG, OKPZ, KP VJG JQRG VJCV AQW'NN IGV VJG EQFG - OKPZ. JG'U PGXGT FQPG VJKU DGHQTG. XGTA YQTTKGF CDQWV OKPZ! Love Sam!'

Isabella quickly closed down the computer and went back to her room. She opened the curtains and could see the message in code quite easily in the ghostly white light.

OKPZ. That comes several times. Could it be Minx, she wondered.

If so O=M, K=I, P=N and Z=X. She looked at it hard.

"Got it! The code's two letters on - so I have to work two letters back."

With shaking hands but speedily, she wrote, 'J, that's H, and C is A, then X is V and G is E.'

She wrote clearly.

'Minx! Have you seen Minx? Minx has gone. I repeat his name, Minx, in the hope that you'll get the code - Minx. He's never done this before. Very worried about Minx!

Love Sam.'

At last, that was it. She looked at the first message and decoded, 'haven't seen Minx since I got on the plane.'

Well that figures, she thought.

She'd better get to work.

And yes, she thought, Minx is about but I haven't actually seen him.

How was she to explain that to Sam?

'Dear Sam,' she wrote,

'I think Minx is here with me - up to all kinds of tricks that I don't like at all - helping me with my tennis, interfering with computers. But I haven't seen him which I think is very cowardly of him, and I wish you'd take him back. See what you can do. For my part, I can only wish him away.

Love Bizzie.'

Carefully, patiently, she wrote it all out by hand in code, returned to the spare room and closed the door. Again Minx's face appeared on the lit screen. Had Isabella's thoughts given him that smirk or was he really grinning? She dismissed him with one press of the E-mail, typed out her coded message and switched off the computer leaving Minx trapped inside.

Over the next few weeks, several more messages passed between Sam and Isabella but no new events arose to shed light on Minx's disappearance, apart from his face on the computer and the occasional bedroom window mysteriously opened. He seemed to have lost interest in tennis completely, for which Isabella was truly grateful.

George and Isabella had won most of their matches against other schools. They'd kept up their consistently good form and were now through to the finals of the junior tennis doubles tournament in their own school. It was a hot day as they went out on to the court to play against Hannah and James. It was going to be a close thing. George and Isabella won the first set 7-5 but were down 4-2 in the second. It was Isabella to serve and she'd been having trouble with her first serve. Again, into the net it went and her second serve dropped nervously just into their opponents' service court. Hannah slammed it back short, angled out of the court on to Isabella's backhand. How could Isabella have got that? It was a winner. From that point on George and Isabella didn't look back. A backhand, then a smash and another smash, so it went on. Isabella seemed to have wings. George was almost embarrassed. Isabella on the other hand was furious. She could hardly fight back the tears of anger as she shook hands with their defeated opponents. She had to face the presentation of the cup.

"Why so modest, Bizzie? Don't hang back." This was followed by the photos with a glowering Isabella and a jubilant George.

After school she deliberately waited so that she could cycle home alone. She felt so ashamed, but what could she do? She couldn't have dropped out of the tennis at that stage. It wouldn't have been fair to George. Thank goodness she was going out to Hong Kong next week. Maybe she and Sam could sort out this whole thing together.

At the end of the week, she collected her tennis photos.

"Hmm!" she looked at herself.

"Not very good of you, Bizzie," said Poppy, peering over her shoulder. "What were you looking like that for?"

Isabella ignored the question.

Back home she threw the photos disgustedly on to the kitchen table.

What a way to win, she thought.

"Ooh Bizzie! What a look!" laughed her mother, perusing the photos. "I thought that look was reserved for when you're annoyed with me - and who's the Chinese boy next to you?"

Isabella's heart sank to the pit of her stomach.

"Where's George?" asked her mum.

Isabella approached her mother's back and looked over her shoulder.

"George - er - George was sick for the photos - and - er - Minx - Michael was reserve - so he stood in," she faltered.

The phone rang and her mother took the call. Isabella stared disbelievingly at the photo. So that was Minx. Minx in full tennis kit.

Well, he deserved to be there, she thought. "He'd won more tennis points than anyone else - but - just you wait Sam. We're going to get this thing sorted out," she muttered, stomping up to her room.

DANGEROUS FRIEND

Chapter 3
Saved Your Life

"Da-ad! Please don't tell me again. You're worse than Mum!" Isabella and her father were in their car going to the airport.

"It's serious stuff Bizzie. You're on your own going halfway round the world - "

"I won't be on my own," retorted Isabella "The plane'll be full of people and the airhostess will be in charge of me. I don't even need an airhostess. And I'll be met by Uncle Justin at the other end."

"You have to be in the care of someone. You're not a teenager yet," said her father.

They parked the car and Isabella was duly delivered to Kathy, the airhostess who was to hand her over to Sam's family in Hong Kong.

"Mum'll join you in ten days, on the Tuesday," said Dad. "Give our love to the family, and help Aunty Charlotte."

"I will." Isabella kissed her father. "See you soon," she called over her shoulder as she went through Immigration.

The airhostess, Kathy, was there to look after her, but even so Isabella felt an exhilarating sense of freedom. She loved airports. They were full of faces - faces! Her heart fluttered for a moment, as Minx's face crossed her mind. Where was he? Could you give a ghost the slip? But she was determined not to let thoughts of

Minx cloud her day. She just loved being on her own and her own boss.

She had a seat by the window on the plane. An Indian man, older than her father, took the seat next to her. It was a clear day, so cloudless that she could see the south coast as the plane flew over it. She was on her way to Hong Kong for a wonderful holiday. Goodbye England! Isabella chatted happily to Mr Patel while all the early bustle of the flight began. You couldn't always follow parents' instructions to the letter. It would be stupid and very rude to sit in silence when she had a friendly neighbour.

"We'd better pay attention to this," said Mr Patel as the screen came down and the safety instructions began.

"Oh dear!" giggled Isabella. "They seem to have put it on fast forward."

The screen was a blur of safety belts and an airhostess talking in a high squeaky voice. Then Kathy, the airhostess in charge of Isabella, went to the front of the plane, obviously to adjust the film. This time it was worse, fast backwards. The passengers were amused. The decision was made to do the safety show in real life. Isabella and Mr Patel watched as Kathy put the safety belt on inside out. Then she got the ties crossed and round one shoulder so that they wouldn't meet. People were now laughing out loud, but they were nervous too, wondering if the rest of the flight would be as confused as the safety display. Kathy was red in the face while the hostess in the opposite aisle looked across at her, half in sympathy and half impatiently.

Happily, it was soon time for drinks and lunch.

"Ugh!" exclaimed Isabella. "Whatever's in this?" she asked as she took the first sip of her coke.

Mr Patel looked at her glass and tried his fresh orange juice, which was just as unpleasant to him. "Mine's got gin in it, and I'm afraid I don't drink alcohol. Let me smell yours," he said to Isabella. "The same! Oh dear, I hope this isn't going to be one of those flights."

Kathy, who had poured the drinks, was very embarrassed, especially as several other passengers around them had the wrong drinks too.

"Oh no!" Isabella let out an audible gasp.

"What is it?" asked Mr Patel.

"Oh - er - nothing," was the reply. It surely couldn't be you-know-who doing all this? She pushed the idea from her mind. No, just a coincidence. People have days when nothing goes right.

Just to be friendly, Isabella found herself telling her Indian friend that she was half Indian.

"And do you follow Hinduism?" he asked.

"Not really, but my mum who's English knows a lot about Indian and Chinese religions," she said

"And do you believe in reincarnation?" he asked.

"It sounds nice, but I don't think so. I don't even believe in hell, just heaven," she said and then added, "but I don't really think about that kind of thing much."

"Oh, it's very interesting," went on her friend, "much more messy and complicated than Christianity. Now where you're going to - China - Hong Kong is part of China, isn't it?"

"Sort of," she replied.

"Many of the Chinese are Buddhist and their Scriptures were brought from India to China by a very wise man called Tripitaka, a Monkey God, Pigsy and a monster called Sandy."

"I've heard that story before," said Isabella, thinking that was another coincidence.

Mr Patel was deeply into religion and he talked for quite a while about it, finding her a willing listener.

Night comes quickly when you're flying to Hong Kong to meet the following day, as it wings its way towards you. Dinner was served - no hitches there - and afterwards there was to be a film with Arnold Schwarzenegger.

Bound to be good, thought Isabella knowing that he was one of Sam's favourites.

She was beginning to feel really at home as she removed her shoes and slipped on the soft socks provided, ready for the evening's movie watching. The film was certainly action-packed. Isabella shivered. The air vent had come on suddenly. Wind through her hair - or had she been touched by the girl behind? She patted the top of her head with her hand and cast a look over her shoulder. The spectre of

Minx was in her head - but was he out there too?

"Do you believe in ghosts, Mr Patel?" she asked. Why had she opened her mouth, she thought in the next moment.

"Of course I do!"

She'd known the answer all along...

"Fat lot of comfort that was!" she thought, snuggling deeper under her blue blanket.

"Yes, I think ghosts are all about us," Mr Patel began.

"Are they good or bad?" Isabella turned her big brown eyes tentatively towards him.

Mr Patel read her anxiety. "Mostly good. I mean there's one Chinese goddess, Kuan Yin, the Goddess of Mercy, who's there between heaven and earth, to help people. And there are other gods, like the Monkey God I told you about earlier, who get sent to earth as a punishment. They ought to be on their best behaviour - though they're not always," he added ruefully. "Then there are just the straightforward people who die and who have things back on earth that bother them - even Christians believe that. Anyway you can feel them about you, can't you?"

Isabella nodded miserably, wishing she'd never introduced the subject.

"I mean this plane. I wasn't going to mention it, but - well - there's a presence here."

Isabella continued to look wide-eyed at her neighbour.

"I think you feel it or you wouldn't have

talked about ghosts - " he paused, "would you?"

"Yes, I do feel it," she admitted shakily. "But I don't want to feel it," and she pressed her lips tightly together.

"Do you like the film?" he asked, more deftly changing the subject.

Isabella wrinkled up her nose. "It's a bit violent for me."

"Me too! But look at that!" Mr Patel and Isabella, along with the rest of the plane, roared with laughter.

Arnold Schwarzenegger, packed with muscle, was on the floor, and every time he tried to get up, he was punched back down again - and again - and again, the same punch, the same expression on his face. The reel was stuck. The atmosphere on the plane was one of great amusement. Poor Kathy appeared once more with apologies. The lights went up. There was to be a Tarzan film.

"Where did they dig that up from?" laughed Mr Patel. "Much more to my taste."

"And mine," agreed Isabella, now a little sleepy.

She managed a gentle snooze through most of Tarzan, but was awakened with a violent start. There was a loud clap of thunder. The captain's voice was ringing through the aeroplane. "Please return to your seats. We might be meeting some turbulence."

The tension in the plane was felt by everyone. It was warm and the plane had begun to bounce around a little. There was the usual creaking and clanking and very unpleasant noises that accompany rough weather. Isabella lifted the blind at her side and as she did so a jagged flash of vivid electricity raced towards her, lighting up the seats nearby in a neon flash. She quickly pulled down the blind. There followed another loud crack juddering the plane fiercely. The last few people were hurrying back to their seats and there was the clunking of seat belts. Isabella tightened hers and Mr Patel leant over to see she was secured. The plane now seemed to be a mere toy for the elements. It bumped erratically and its stability was being put to the test alarmingly.

"There is a jinx on this flight." Mr Patel grinned, seeing that Isabella was looking pale.

Her eyes opened wide. Not a jinx - but could it - could it be - Minx - she thought, tightening her grip on the arm rest.

She had no time to ponder this. A flash of light cut through the blind followed immediately by a huge crash and roll of thunder. The storm seemed to be all around them. Then she felt as if she had left her stomach behind as the plane dropped like a stone, continuing its descent with colossal bounces. Suddenly their passage became smoother, but all the lights on the plane had gone out. There was pandemonium amongst the passengers, some of whom had screamed at the drop. Almost everyone was talking, shouting, some were crying - relief at the unexpected calm. In the horror, Isabella found herself clutching on to Mr Patel's hand. She had never felt so afraid. She waited for the calm voice of the captain saying that all was well.

"The electrics have been hit," said Mr Patel, "so the captain won't be able to get through to speak to us."

The calm of their flight now seemed assured, and slowly the airhostesses re-emerged from their seats, providing drinks and friendly reassurance. They held torches and they too were white and shaken. It seemed the plane was to make an unscheduled landing in Agra. Everyone was encouraged to stay calm. The landing was surprisingly smooth and the passengers clapped, but as they peered into the velvet Indian night they saw the flashing of the lights of fire engines. They disembarked the quick way down, the chute. There was a jumble of people at the bottom of the chute. Isabella found Mr Patel and helped him to his feet. They were rushed to waiting buses which took off immediately for the safety of the airport. When they looked back they could see that the tail of the plane had caught fire but was now under control. Back on the safety of land, Isabella had just begun to enjoy the adventure once more. She preferred action to the terror of wondering and waiting. They were to spend the next twenty four hours at a hotel in Agra waiting for another plane to arrive.

She opened the curtain of her room in the hotel on the fifth floor. She gasped, for there below was a floating dreamy-white temple lit up in the moonlight. She knew it was the Taj Mahal. She thought it perfect. Its presence took her breath away, filling her with reverence and wonder. Her own sigh brought her back to the room and her plight. It had been a strange few hours; all the trivial amusing happenings at the start of the journey; the fun of the film; and finally, almost total disaster. Even the crew had been taken by surprise by the storm because the captain said there was no evidence of it on the radar. It had really been a bolt from the blue.

Involuntarily her heart began to pound, racing ahead of her thoughts. Surely not! But Mr Patel had felt a presence too. Could Minx have been responsible for the fun at the outset and for the terrifying events of the storm? Minx was transformed from an amusing, annoying phantom that was only just out of her control, to a ghostly force that heralded danger - danger directly to her life. Her heart missed a beat. She looked around the bare room, its only decoration a picture of an alien-faced dancer, with heavily made-up, unseeing eyes. But she was all right. Safe here in Agra, Kathy in the adjoining room, waiting for a telephone call from her mother, her life saved.

'Saved your life!' She could hear Sam's voice now. Her lips broadened into a smile as she remembered the trick Sam used to play on her when they were younger.

Just like Sam, she thought as she imagined Sam clutching her from behind pretending to push her under a bus, only to retrieve her at the last moment, screeching,

'Saved your life! Ha! Ha! Ha!'

Was that what Minx was doing - putting me in and then saving my life - trying to impress me? She looked around the poorly lit room again. She jumped as the phone rang.

"Mum!" she called, wiping back a few unwanted tears. "No, I'm okay - honest, but it was a bit scary!" She paused.

"No don't be silly. What could you do here? - sit and hold my hand?"

Again she waited, more composed now, for her mother's anxious comments.

"We're only going to be here for a day. Kathy's really nice - and Judith, she's the other airhostess - oh and Mr Patel - "

Clearly her mother didn't like the sound of Mr Patel.

"He's really super," Isabella assured her mother, "and we're going to see an Indian temple after dinner." Pause.

"No, no, really you'd like him. He's very religious! And he knows the captain. He travels regularly on Cathay Pacific going to Hong Kong on business." Again she waited.

"Yes, do phone Aunty Charlotte - yes - love you too - and by the way - you'll be green - I can see the Taj Mahal from my bedroom window - yes, it's dreamy! - bye - see you a week on Tuesday. I will! I will!" Isabella was back to her usual buoyant self as she called Kathy to have a final word which her mother had insisted upon.

Outside the streets were full of people selling everything under the sun. No one seemed to have a home and all activities were done by the side of the road. There was every kind of transport, from clapped out buses to weird looking black taxis, to pedicabs and donkeys and camels. There was other animal life on the streets too: goats, horses, chickens, ducks, and of course the sacred cow, which did as it pleased. There was bustle, colours, smells, and Isabella loved it.

Mr Patel was accompanying Isabella, together with her two escorts, Kathy and Judith to a Buddhist temple. As they pushed and jostled their way through the hot, crowded streets, Isabella had a wonderful feeling that the whole world was there with her. But people were poor, she could see that.

They approached a large, white, domed building. There were many people on the steps leading up to it. The four climbed up and approached the wide doorway. It was crowded inside and rhythmically noisy. So many colours amidst an air of deep concentration. Everyone was sitting cross-legged on the floor, chanting and banging bells together. Their heads were bowed. Mr Patel motioned his three charges to the side of the huge room where they also sat.

It was cooler inside the temple but Isabella found the atmosphere oppressive. The chanting and the ringing seemed to be inside her head. She felt afraid, panicky. She noticed that many people around her were suddenly looking in her direction, their concentration broken. They looked at her with large liquid eyes that mirrored her own. The chanting became faster, and the accompanying ringing louder, and more rhythmically insistent. The people seemed to be aware of - of - something outside themselves, ghostly and powerful. Mr Patel looked alarmed too, and rose to his feet. Isabella stood up at the same moment and staring straight in front of her amidst the gathering sound, she said aloud,

"I do believe in reincarnation."

In that second, a gentle breeze ruffled her curls and before her, shimmeringly, Minx slowly appeared to her. Had he appeared to other people? They were certainly aware of his presence, just as Mr Patel had been on the plane. Now total panic overcame Isabella. She ran towards the doorway, half falling over the chanting crowd. Down the white steps she sped avoiding the small groups of worshippers, meditators, beggars, happy people, lonely ones. She was out in the world, alone and afraid.

She was breathing hard but she ran on, not knowing where. Instead of the busy faces, preoccupied with themselves, she saw strange faces wearing masks, painted faces, contorted faces, laughing and jeering at her. Many of them were on floats. They laughed grotesquely and threw paint on her. Her blouse, her hair, her trousers were a cacophony of iridescent paint. She couldn't get away from them. Every corner she turned found her among more weird, more alien surroundings, which blurred into each other in her head. But then she came upon a narrow alleyway, deserted. She ran to the end. It was dark, not lit in any way and it became darker the more she escaped from the horrors of the noise and the pressure of the crowds. At last she came to a halt, panting and half sobbing. She crouched in a filthy doorway and leant against the closed door. Her heart was pounding.

"No! No!" she shrieked, pressing against the scratches on the door. It gave way and she found herself in an open corridor from where she could see the stars above.

But Minx was there, following her inside. Minx, whom she could see again now, there but ghostly, not real as Sam had made out. She momentarily wondered if this was how Sam saw Minx, so used to him that he ignored the shimmering uncertain outline. Minx held out a finely-boned thin white hand. She recoiled against the mouldy walls. He came and stood right beside her, quite still; then he insistently took her right hand. Resistance seemed futile.

Quite silently, he led her back along the

deserted alley into the streets. But now they appeared to be only normally busy for India. The faces were again happy and preoccupied. She followed her companion helplessly. Minx stopped to stroke a cow. Isabella almost smiled. He stole some delicious spicy meat and vegetables on a skewer, cooked on an open charcoal fire. That was her first thought back to the humdrum of her old life - her mother would certainly not have approved of her enjoying this tasty morsel. Then hand in hand, they stood still at the entrance to a huge marquee. There was singing, clapping, more banging of bells, but now the scene no longer oppressed her. Dancers in bright costumes, large-eyed, flashed around a large stage. This was a world apart, a world she began to enjoy with Minx, her ghostly friend; a world of colour, eyes and noise, whose meaning she had ceased trying to grasp. She felt peaceful, tired, not unhappy, at one with the face of India.

The pair turned a corner. The Taj Mahal rose, splendid, white in the moonlight. The hotel was in sight. As she walked through the swing doors, she was met by the desperate face of Kathy who fell on her and wept with relief. There were recriminations, affirmations, a lot of commotion. Fortunately no one as yet had phoned her parents. It all seemed to Isabella in her present state of mind, that the worry was quite out of proportion. She noted too that no one, not even Mr Patel, could see Minx.

She slept a deep, faraway sleep, unaware that Kathy came to check on her several times during the night. The sun streamed in through open curtains when she awoke. Minx was at the window looking at the Taj Mahal. He turned to her and smiled, an earthly smile that belied the vagueness of his dress and outline. It seemed that wherever he was, he took on the mode of dress around him so that even to an independent observer, he tended to blend into the scene.

Isabella was given breakfast in bed. She was being treated like some sort of invalid who had had a brainstorm. She found this infuriating and wouldn't stand for it. As the door of her room closed and her breakfast tray disappeared down the corridor, she jumped squarely off the bed.

"Now, look here Minx!" she began, sounding alarmingly like herself. "What was all that about the terrible storm? There was no trace of it on the radar system - it was all manufactured by you - " She glared at him. His shape took on a sylphlike form and his expression was one of complete indifference. He looked back at the Taj Mahal, seemingly captivated by it.

Isabella was exasperated.

"You create - mayhem - near disaster - and then you roll up - knight in shining armour - and save me from a fate worse than death. You know all about 'Saved your life' from Sam, I know - and you've been playing just that trick!"

She paused.

"I'm going to have it out with Sam. You're his - his friend - and you can have fun and games together but you must leave me out of it. Do you hear?" she shouted loudly.

Minx got down from the window. Calmly, he closed her large suitcase, opened the door and put it on the waiting trolley. Isabella had no choice but to follow him down the passageway, onto the lift, down to the foyer below where she met the rest of the passengers. Mr Patel took charge of her and within a couple of hours they were once more in the blue above the clouds, happily bound for Hong Kong.

Chapter 4
One Pair of Eyes

Isabella fastened her seat belt ready for landing, looking enchantedly out of the aeroplane window. She felt she could almost touch the tops of the skyscrapers in Kowloon. How did the pilot find his way down to Kai Tak Airport through that jungle of tall buildings? She felt a great sense of anticipation. She had always been deeply sensitive to changes in her immediate surroundings but now there was an additional dimension to her life which was not at all welcome. Minx was sitting in the middle of the plane between two large ladies. She turned to give him a dirty look which was meant to ensure that he behaved himself.

"No jinx on this plane," said Mr Patel who was sitting beside her.

"We haven't landed yet," said Isabella only half laughing.

"It's such an exciting airport to fly into. I always think we're not going to make it, or that we're going to slide off the runway into the sea."

Isabella said goodbye to Mr Patel and went with Kathy through to Immigration. She couldn't help being amused at Minx. It was rather like having a very efficient husband around, she smiled to herself. He always managed to lead her - and so Kathy too - to the shortest queue, and he was an expert with wayward trollies.

Sam and his dad waved furiously as she and Minx made their grand entrance down the ramp to join all the people who were there to meet friends and relatives. She thanked Kathy and ran to meet Sam. His eyes gave her a piercing questioning look, so she knew he couldn't see Minx who was standing right beside him, watching his every movement. She looked over her shoulder meaningfully, but couldn't enlighten Sam more than that, because her uncle was there. Naturally, both he and Sam were keen to hear the story of the storm and the damaged plane.

Sam and Isabella sat in the back of the car while Sam's dad drove through the teeming streets of Kowloon. She was careful to leave a big space by her for Minx which gave Sam some information at least. He stared at the seemingly empty corner by the window and shrugged his shoulders which told Isabella quite a lot too. Clearly, handing Minx back to his - his owner, was not going to be that easy. She felt troubled.

Isabella gazed down from her cousin's flat on the Peak on the north side of Hong Kong Island. She could see the airport across the harbour and beyond the blue of the sea to Lantau Island. Again, the tops of buildings in the bustling city were almost within her reach, but there were trees and bushes too, lots of green to contrast sharply with the man-made concrete which made up much of Hong Kong. Amazingly, it was a magical sight, full of drama.

It was clear that she and Sam were not going to have a minute together that day. Sophie and BeBe were full of news.

"BeBe's in love!" declared Sophie. "He's a wimp of course."

"No, he's not," retorted BeBe. "He's gorgeous. You're just jealous!"

"Jealous! Don't make me laugh!" But she did laugh. "He just moons around her all day. It's very boring."

"Bit of green eye alright," interjected Sam. "But Soph's right, he is a wimp!"

And with that both sisters laid into their brother. One thing about Sam, he was always fair - equally scathing about both sisters!

The following day Sam managed to prize Isabella out of the clutches of the family. She was keen to talk too and to give Minx back to his rightful owner. Since their arrival in Hong Kong, Minx's behaviour had been distinctly low key. For reasons of his own, he seemed to want to keep a low profile, although he had caused one great upset which gave Isabella further unease. Sam and his cousin were walking, tennis racquets in hand, through the thick Peak foliage down the hillside to the tennis club. Minx walked by Isabella making gestures from time to time that he'd like to carry her kit. She ignored him.

"You know that ink on the tablecloth was Minx." Isabella turned to look at her cousin.

"I guessed as much," said Sam sounding slightly dejected. "Why would he want to get me into trouble? He's never been like this before."

"Search me," she said. "I can only think he's trying to - sort of - break with you."

"Is he with you all the time?" asked Sam.

Isabella nodded, the expression on her face indicating that this was not a situation she sought.

"Like you said, though, I'm not really aware of him all the time. I'm bothered that you can't make contact with him. You know I was counting on you to put him in his place."

Isabella recounted once more the details of the events on the plane.

"You know it was a clear case of 'Saved your life'!" she finished.

Sam grinned at her. "He's trying to impress you, isn't he?"

"Looks like it. And it was very dangerous. I don't mind admitting I was terrified in that storm, and so was everyone else on the plane." "He's got worse," said Sam shaking his head. "I'm beginning to wish I'd never told you."

"Gee thanks! How do you think I feel? I mean, you've had a - a - a friend, a shadow all your life - so you must be used to it - but I like my freedom. I need to be on my own sometimes. I'm a free spirit."

Isabella could see that she was sounding ridiculously dramatic, but she was beginning to feel very frustrated that Sam seemed to have no more power over Minx than she had.

"And I don't want to be impressed," she added. "Let's sit down for a mo'."

They had arrived at a shady bench.

"Look Sam," she said, patting the bench for him to sit next to her.

Sam had a look on his face that said, 'what now?'

"You know when you first told me about Minx, I thought it was all in your head." She cast a glance in the direction of Minx.

He appeared to be oblivious of their conversation and was examining a leaf in minute detail. Minx had this way of assuming an air of total distraction when he smelt trouble.

"And now what do you think?" Sam looked at his cousin challengingly.

"I think you're not crazy, not infantile or any of those things that might make you need a friend who never leaves your side. I think now that Minx is - a ghost. What else can he be? But why he should have chosen you to haunt - and now me, unfortunately - I've no idea."

There was silence as Sam struggled with this new notion.

"I think you've got a real cheek, Bizz," he said at last. "You come along, a complete newcomer to Minx - "

"No I did not just 'come along' as you say. You dragged me into this - and if I'd known where it was going to lead, I'd have been kicking and screaming."

"Well anyway, you are a complete newcomer - and instead of accepting Minx's friendship, you start analysing and interpreting his nature, dissecting him, as if he were an object - an object in a lab. He's a friend. He's kind. Well, he's usually kind and I'd like to have him back."

"You're welcome to have him back, but he shows no sign of wanting to leave," she shouted, continuing the quarrel. "And I think he's dangerous - to me at any rate. What would have happened if his silly - 'Saved your life' game had gone wrong?"

"Don't let's quarrel, Bizz." Sam's experience with two older sisters had taught him that quarrelling with women was a futile task. They always had the last word. And in any case his naturally good nature didn't like being in conflict, especially not with people he liked.

"Tell you what, Bizzie, let's not mention him unless it's necessary."

Isabella nodded.

"But if something does - er - happen, you can give me a bulletin."

"Okay. Tennis then?"

"Tennis," he agreed.

They played two sets of singles. Sam was quite glad when they were over. Isabella had won the first set 6-4 and the second 6-1. Minx had been slow to join in, but once the game was underway he was there to the fore, annoying Isabella almost as much as her cousin.

"I can't see any point in playing if he's going to help you all the time," complained Sam.

"I like that!" Isabella could see the funny side. "You've had Minx's help all your life - Sam the great sportsman, and now you're complaining when he's helping the other side."

It wasn't as easy to ignore Minx as they had thought.

"Yes, but he's actually hindering me. Although I can't see him, I can feel it. He's not just helping you. You've got a double advantage."

"So what do we do, give up tennis?"

"Oh no!" Sam agreed they'd just have to put up with Minx and hope he'd get tired of wanting to join in.

"What do you think we should do about the Junior Tournament?" Isabella asked. She had been so looking forward to it. "Do you think it's fair to enter?" she went on, remembering the fiasco she'd gone through at school only a few days ago.

"Seems fair," said Sam, "after all, Minx might be on your side, but he's certainly mucking my game up."

He didn't want to miss the tournament either.

"Have a talk to him," suggested Isabella. "Tell him not to interfere," she said, taking a sip of her orange juice.

She took out her book. "I won't listen, honest! He's leaning over the balcony by the big plant, watching the game below."

Sam approached the spot where he thought Minx was. He looked over his shoulder to see that no one was in earshot. Isabella could see her cousin's face assume a most serious look. His lips moved and he appeared to be giving Minx a lecture of the kind he frequently received himself. She couldn't help smiling.

Over the next week, Sam and Isabella played the preliminary rounds of their tennis tournament. She was playing brilliantly, with the help of Minx of course. For Sam it was another story. The day of the final arrived and Minx ensured that they would be taking part. Isabella's heart sank as she removed the cover from her racquet. Surely it wasn't going to be a repetition of her last final when she and George had emerged in all their glory.

Sam was not playing badly, but Isabella was playing brilliantly, everyone agreed. She had to try her best or Minx's part in the game would have been plain for all to see. They won the first set 6-3. Their opponents were no mean players.

"Why aren't you coming up to the net when you've served?" asked Isabella as they changed ends.

"Well I don't think it fair to have three people at the net," he shrugged. "And is it necessary? After all, you and Minx are pretty impossible to pass as it is."

In the second set, Sam and Isabella were at odds. There were lots of calls of 'yours' and 'mine'. There were many misunderstandings when they clashed, racquets in midair, going for the same ball. Isabella broke a string and went to the side of the court to change her racquet. She'd have to play with Sophie's. Minx was at her side fussing away.

"Cut it out, Minx! Leave me alone! Let me play my own game," she muttered through clenched teeth. "I'm fed up with you."

Sam and Isabella were 4-1 down when play began again. But then she couldn't put a foot wrong. Sam was furious and embarrassed to the point where he had almost stopped trying.

"He's not helping me!" hissed Isabella.

"You - what?"

"He's on the top diving board, sulking. I'm on my own," she grinned.

"All right then," said Sam, suddenly fused with renewed energy.

The next serve was his, a good one. He made a dash to the net and delivered an unplayable smash. Sam's next serve was driven back over the net, but Isabella returned it with a low chop. The ball dropped just over the net. They were inspired, especially Isabella who felt exhilarated at her new-found freedom.

72

This time she enjoyed the presentation, feeling that they had deserved the cup, more or less. She was reluctant to be photographed but as far as she could tell, Minx had remained pouting and surveying the events from the top diving board.

"Why so modest?" asked Sophie of her young cousin. "Enjoy the glory. I did. It doesn't happen often."

"It doesn't happen to me at all," said BeBe who was no great tennis player.

"You're good at other things, BeeBs," said Isabella. "Like making everyone fall in love with you," she laughed.

"Oh that!" said BeBe ruefully. "That doesn't count!"

They were in the changing room, preparing to go down town to have their fortunes told.

"It's great fun," said Sophie. "You can't come to Hong Kong and not look into your future."

"Is Sam coming?" asked Isabella.

"Oh, I expect he'll tag along, but you'll never get him to show his palm. Says it's all rubbish."

"It probably is," said BeBe. "But it's fun. Why is it boys don't like fun? Hey Sophie - cut it out!"

"What?" asked Sophie innocently.

"Whipping off my towel!" said the naked BeBe.

"I didn't, honest!" laughed Sophie. "What would I want to do that for?"

Isabella could see that it had been Minx's work. She glared at him as he now stood behind Sophie looking at her in the mirror.

"BeBe, don't!" Sophie shouted at her sister who she thought had ruffled her freshly spiked hair.

Fortunately BeBe ignored her and Isabella gave Minx another dirty look, as she led the way out of the changing room as fast as she could.

"Let's walk down town," Sophie suggested. "It'll be quicker than waiting for the bus. You coming Sam?"

"Suppose I'd better - "

"Don't be a martyr. We'll be perfectly okay on our own," retorted BeBe.

"I'm not doing anything, I'll come," said Sam. "But it is a waste of money. He charges, you know, Bizz!"

"Not much," said Sophie. "I'll treat you Bizzie. It's a real laugh."

"Can he speak English?" asked Isabella.

"No, but we'll translate for you," BeBe replied.

"How come you two can speak Cantonese and Sam can't?" she asked.

"Because they had an amah who spoke to them all the time - and they talk to some of their Chinese friends at school. And they used to watch Chinese TV a lot. Trouble was, by the time I came along, the amah had had it up to here," Sam said putting his hand to the top of his head, "with these two and so she left!"

"No she didn't. You had her until you were three, but you were a slow learner. Anyway I'm glad I can speak Chinese. It's handy."

The four of them walked further down the

hillside into the thick of the western district.

"It's noisy!" said Isabella. "How do they live with such a din?" she asked as they passed a pile driver, then a restaurant where the constant click of mahjong tiles could be heard. And above everything there was the noise of buses, cars, trams, hooting, laughter, talking. They made their way with some difficulty along the crowded streets to a small temple. Two large wooden guardians, eyes popping out of their heads, making fearful faces, stood guard. Isabella made a face back and giggled with Sam who was watching her. Sophie wrinkled up her nose and shook her head.

"You have to be serious from now on. He's a Taoist priest and very holy," she whispered.

BeBe led the way inside. It was dark except for a few dusty rays of sunshine slanting through the doorway and a dozen or so candles at the altar. There was the strong, mysterious smell of joss sticks.

"What are all these?" asked Isabella pointing to the many stone statues.

"They're gods," said BeBe quietly.

"And there's a white tiger round here." Isabella was snooping around. "He looks as if he's hiding."

"Be careful. He's a 'cher san'. You worship him to keep on the right side of him," explained Sophie.

"Yes." BeBe's big blue eyes were almost popping out of her head.

She was already beginning to absorb the atmosphere. It never failed to get to her.

Sophie motioned to them all to buy a candle which they stuck in the sand on the altar. They all bowed their heads reverently as she did.

"Now we must find the priest." Sophie led the way to the back of the temple.

In spite of the din outside, it was curiously quiet when they went deeper inside.

They said, "Jo san", to a thin man in priest's robes and he pointed to the wooden chair in front of him.

"Cheng chor," he said to Sophie. He recognised her.

First of all he scrutinised her face with his small slanting eyes which were surrounded by many upturned wrinkles. He had a kind face. Then he pushed back her hair revealing her ears. He looked long and hard. Isabella tried hard not to look at Sam. She noted that Minx had disappeared.

Perhaps it's just as well, she thought. We don't want him putting a spanner in the works - making himself known to the priest.

Then the priest took Sophie's hand and turned up her palm.

Finally, he smiled.

"Geet fan," he said in a satisfied way.

"Gay si?" asked Sophie.

"Luk neen," he replied. "Geet fan. Herng fuk. Ho dor sai lo gor!" he pronounced.

"Gay dor sai lo gor?" Sophie questioned him

once more.

He laughed, "Waak jek - mm - luk sap!"

Sophie cast a look at BeBe who grinned.

"What does he say?" asked Isabella. "Is it good?"

"It depends on what you call good," said Sophie. "He says I'm going to get married in about six years' time, and have five, six, seven children, maybe! Go on, BeBe. It's your turn."

"No you," said BeBe suddenly nervous, looking at her cousin.

"No BeeBs. He says you." Sophie was insistent.

BeBe took the chair and looked down modestly, revealing her long sweeping eyelashes.

"Mm hai," said the priest. "Tai ngor la."

BeBe raised her eyes and looked at the priest's wrinkled brown face.

It was a nice face, she thought, like those paintings you see of gnarled old Chinese men in the tourist shops.

Again he stared into her eyes and swept her hair behind her ears to survey them. He shook his head but his face still had a friendly air.

"Dor yan serng sum," he said, followed by another longer sentence.

BeBe couldn't help looking at her older sister. They both laughed and the priest smiled too in a kind way. He added another phrase in Cantonese.

"I'll have to come to sponge off you, Sophie," said BeBe, getting up and making way for Isabella.

In answer to her cousin's questioning face, Sophie said, "BeBe's going to leave a trail of broken hearts, and then she's going to marry the poorest! Just like BeeBs. He's got her right."

Isabella sat down before the priest. She noticed that Sam had now disappeared, as well as Minx. Maybe they were together. She resented the responsibility she felt for Minx, always worried that he might produce another 'Saved your life' situation. The priest's face changed as he gazed into Isabella's dark eyes. His face became more wrinkled than ever. He pushed back her brown-black curls then covered them quickly. She held out her palm, but he shook his head. Isabella felt a familiar pang of panic. She looked from one to the other of her cousins.

"Gan loy msu fuk?" asked the priest.

"He wants to know if you've been off colour lately," said Sophie.

Isabella was unsure of how to reply.

"I had a slight tummy upset," she began. "I'm not used to the food here."

Sophie passed the information on to the priest.

"He wants you to write down your name and date of birth," she continued, while the priest handed a piece of paper and a brush to Isabella.

"He's going to do an eight character reading."

"What's that?" asked Isabella alarmed. "Is something wrong?"

"No, No! It's all right. He's going to write down your name in Chinese characters. I don't understand how it works, but it has something to do with your date of birth as well."

The priest looked hard at the characters he had taken from Isabella's name. He spoke in a whisper to Sophie so that Isabella couldn't hear. Sophie looked from him to BeBe back to her young cousin. "He says there's someone from the other world trying to get in touch with you."

Isabella sighed deeply. Was he aware of Minx, she wondered. And where on earth is Minx anyway?

She looked around her rather grubby surroundings. The priest continued his explanation to Sophie and BeBe who looked distinctly uncomfortable.

"Now what?" Isabella asked them once more.

The two girls hesitated, neither wanting to tell her.

BeBe put her hand on Isabella's shoulder. "It's just that there's a ghost who wants to marry you," she said softly. "A sort of ghost marriage."

"They often have ghost marriages here in Hong Kong," added Sophie.

"Marry me!" exclaimed Isabella. "Does that mean I have to die so that I can become a ghost?" She sounded afraid, but indignant too.

Was this Minx? Again she thought of him, looking about her uneasily.

Sophie and BeBe piled on several more questions as they stood either side of the old man. And finally they emerged with comforting information.

"He's going to fix it," said BeBe.

"Fix for me to get married to a ghost?" flashed Isabella.

"No, no! Keep calm!" Sophie took Isabella's arm.

She paid the priest and instructed BeBe to get Sam.

She led Isabella out into the noise and sunlight, and squinting at her cousin said, "Don't look so worried. He's going to fix it - he's going to get in touch with another ghost and arrange a marriage. We can be present if you like!"

"No fear! It might not work," said Isabella "and the ghost might prefer me!"

Sophie laughed. "It could be fun. I've heard that they give paper wedding presents like cars and double beds and wardrobes. Then they burn them as a sacrifice to the gods."

"It's weird, I think," Isabella said, glad to be back in the crowded street. BeBe joined them followed by Sam and a reluctant Minx.

He must have felt at home in there, thought Isabella.

Out in the sunlight Isabella suddenly realised that Sam's face was as white as a sheet.

"What's wrong?" she asked him, turning her head away from her older cousins.

Sam shook his head and momentarily grasped her hand. It felt horribly cold. "Later!" he whispered.

"What did you make of all that?" asked

BeBe, looking a little worriedly at Isabella.

"Weird!" Isabella responded. "Do you think there's anything for me to be anxious about?"

"No, I don't think so!" said Sophie, wishing on the quiet that they hadn't brought Isabella to the temple.

"Nothing like that's ever happened before though," began BeBe, deflecting a glare from her sister.

"He'll fix it though, I know," Sophie reassured her cousin.

"What's all this about?" asked Sam, who was slowly beginning to look more like himself.

"A ghost!" exclaimed Isabella. "A bloomin' old ghost wants to marry me! Take me to heaven or wherever - "

"But the priest's going to arrange for somebody who's already up in heaven to marry Isabella's ghost, there's nothing to worry about," said BeBe, noticing that her brother and cousin seemed to be exchanging glances.

"Quite honestly," said Sophie. "I don't believe a word of it - well," she mused, " - or I almost don't. I just take it as a warning. Be like me Bizzie. I do believe that life's mapped out for us to some extent - but I also believe in free will - I can change things now that I've been warned."

"She's going to get married, live happily ever after and have seven children!" chuckled Isabella.

"Imagine it!" said Sophie. "I mean there's a contradiction in those statements! That's the kind of thing I wanted when I was four or five. I think that's what he must have been picking up. No fear! Not now! Be like me Bizzie - warned!"

Sam and Isabella parted from Sophie and BeBe with some relief, leaving them in town to meet up with their boyfriends. They boarded the Peak tram for home.

"Whatever was wrong with you when you came out of the temple?" Isabella at last was able to talk to Sam in private.

"Bizzie, it was terrible," said Sam quietly.

She looked intently at him, then out over the slanting countryside to the harbour. The tram was creaking its way slowly up the very steep slope. Minx was standing by the driver.

"Get back Minx," she called.

Several passengers looked in her direction and so did Minx.

"We don't want any of his tricks," she said.

Amazingly Minx came and sat down behind the pair.

"Well, what happened?" she asked again.

"As soon as we got into the temple, I felt something funny. For one, I'm pretty sure the priest saw Minx - did you notice right at the start?"

Isabella shook her head. "No, but almost the moment we got in there, I realised that Minx had disappeared. I didn't know if he was nosing around in the back or if he was just not visible to me all of a sudden."

"I went into the back, two rooms behind where you were. It was dark and a bit smelly. I noticed there was a Monkey God in one corner. I'm always curious about his hat - you know the one he wears as a punishment - "

She nodded.

"I went over to him and suddenly realised that Minx had got there before me."

"You could see him?"

"Yes. Minx was looking at the Monkey God very intently. He saw me coming over to it," he continued.

"What did he do?" she asked.

"He stood between me and the Monkey God. I knew I shouldn't go any nearer.
He looked - sort of - menacing - " Sam was watching Isabella's face. "Then he went to stand behind the Monkey and put his hand on the Monkey's shoulder. And then it happened." Sam looked terrified.

"What? What?"

"The Monkey God split - he split - fanned out into a myriad of gods. A whole span of faces was there, one behind the other on either side of the original god. They were juddering, shaking, shimmering. They looked at me with - with - hatred - or was it - fear? I don't know." He paused and again his face mirrored the horror he had seen.

"It was then that I started to back away - and then I bumped into BeBe. And after that - that was when you saw me - immediately after. I imagine I must have looked very shaken."

"You sure did! But Minx was behind you

then. He looked rather sorry to be leaving the temple, but he wasn't worked up," she said.

"When I got outside, back into the street, I looked about for Minx and when I couldn't see him, I thought he must be still inside the temple."

"No. He was there following you. That's when I saw him again."

"The Monkey God," Isabella was thinking. "I keep hearing about him. He's supposed to have helped Tripitaka a long time ago."

"Baka Do," said the driver.

The pair rose to leave the tram.

They walked along the leafy road homewards followed at some distance by Minx.

"You know what I think," said Sam.

Isabella turned to him.

"I think that Minx can only be seen by one person at a time."

"Why do you think that?" she asked.

"Because when we went into the temple, you couldn't see him, which I didn't know at the time, but the fortune-teller could. Later when I was getting close to the Monkey God, Minx appeared to me. The fortune-teller presumably was concentrating on you three - you still couldn't see him. Don't you see? Only one pair of eyes. It's a kind of protection thing."

Isabella pondered. "Maybe you've discovered something. And you remember, you couldn't see him when I could - in India."

"You're right Bizz. I admit it! Minx is a ghost."

"Things are never going to be the same again

- that's what I think. Do you think Minx has left you for good?" Isabella questioned.

"And joined you?" he laughed.

"I hope not! Maybe he'll just go to heaven - or some other place between heaven and earth."

"That's where he is now, isn't it? You can't really say he's of this world. You know it sounds disloyal - after all he's been a friend all my life - but I'm nearly thirteen. I should be able to live without a guardian angel," he smiled ruefully. "It would be nice to be on Kuan Yin's list, so she could pop up and help when necessary!"

Isabella laughed. "But I'm too old to get used to a guardian angel. Minx can be a great guy and all that but he can also be very, very naughty - and I think dangerous too."

"Do you really think he's dangerous?" Sam asked.

"Of course he is! Think of the plane."

"And if he's in love with you - maybe he wants you in his world - a ghost marriage and all that!"

Isabella looked very fed up.

"I think you like him being in love with you," grinned Sam.

"Sure, sure! But what makes you think he is?"

"Well, all that drooling around on the top diving board - sulking after you'd told him off. He shows all the signs - and then the fortune-teller said so - or more or less."

Isabella shivered. "But I don't think he's

dangerous only to me! I mean, you're a rival for my attention. My tennis partner no less! My best friend - just about."

"Well, I certainly didn't feel he was my pal any longer - not in the temple. You could be right. But which one of us is it? Which one is in danger?"

"Who knows? Maybe both. But I don't want to be a ghost - and I'm not going to be one! Like Sophie said, I have my own free will. So there Minx! You and your one pair of eyes! Let them not be mine!"

Chapter 5
Very Old Friends

It was unusual for the whole family to be in the kitchen together having breakfast. Sam was last in, sauntering, hands in the back pockets of his jeans, singing that well-known tune, the Wedding March. BeBe picked it up in a flash and jumped up to push Sam to the floor. Sophie almost as quickly joined the fray. Poor Sam was pummelled to death until his mother brought them to order with piercing shouts of "Sophie! BeBe!".

"Mum, you're always on Sam's side!"

Of course Sam had forgotten all about BeBe's recent romance and about Sophie's future with several children. Isabella had known it was directed at her but hadn't dared to give Sam his just desserts. She merely looked on with satisfaction at her older cousins' onslaught.

Sam is the limit, she thought. All this love stuff with Minx could be dangerous - still, I suppose it's better to take a lighthearted view - but I need to be wary too.

Sam was always like this in the mornings, full of excess energy. His mother said it was all downhill from the moment he put his foot out of bed. Today was again sunny. The family was going to Repulse Bay for a beach barbecue. Sam was full of jibes at Isabella.

"Better wear your school regulation swimming cos'. I mean your bikini might be dangerous!"

Isabella took every moment when they were alone to give him a swipe. Definitely the wet towel treatment for him if he went on like this.

"Does he kiss you when you're alone?" Sam asked, only to have his question ignored.

"And where does he go to when you're in the shower?"

This gave Isabella cause for thought.

"I've no idea - I don't look!" she said, adding, "but Minx did whip BeBe's towel off in the girls' changing room."

"Oh well, BeBe's fair game! She just asks to be teased."

They all piled into the station wagon, Sam and Isabella with Molly, the black Labrador squashed together in the back. It wasn't far to the beach. They were to meet the boyfriends there. A quick swim to cool off and then there was rounders. Isabella got a rounder every time she faced the ball - Minx was good at rounders too, and as Isabella whispered to Sam, seemed to be in high spirits. Sam felt a little envious that he couldn't share Minx with his cousin. Minx enjoying himself had always been such fun for Sam. But he was glad at least that Minx was behaving himself.

Sam's mum suggested a sandcastle competition.

"Mum, we're not five!"

Sophie, BeBe and boyfriends set off for a walk along the beach.

"Just look at that!" exclaimed Isabella. "It's lovely."

A junk with orange sails had just arrived in the bay, well beyond the swimming boundary.

"It's going to anchor," said Sam as he watched the sails collapsing.

He peered out to sea. "I think there are only a couple of people on board."

"Let's swim to it," Isabella suggested.

"It's quite a way you know," said Sam's dad. "Are you all right for that distance?"

"Yes, I'm sure I am. The sea's like a millpond. It's good to have a target. Can I - please?"

"Well, all right," said her uncle. "But you must keep close by her, Sam."

The pair waded through the clear shallow water, feeling the soft warm sand beneath their feet. The water was warm and smooth and so refreshing.

"You could lie in this and just go to sleep," said Isabella, lying back, her head almost submerged, her arms and legs outstretched. "Bliss!"

"Is he around?" Sam asked.

"Who? Oh Minx!" Isabella looked about her. "Of course. Seems to be a strong swimmer too!"

"Yep! Any sport our Minx has got taped. You should see him climb trees. There he really does excel!"

Isabella was cutting through the water with a relaxed breaststroke and although Sam was a much stronger swimmer, he dutifully crawled by her side.

"I always think it's creepy when you can't see the bottom - aah!" she screamed.

"What's wrong?" Sam was all concern.

"That so and so Minx, he just pulled my foot!"

"Oh, only him," laughed Sam. "You know we get sharks here sometimes."

"I don't believe you."

"Honest! But not usually at this time of year. And you get warnings from the newspaper and radio - and the lifeguard!"

"Good job Mum doesn't know what I'm doing."

They were well beyond the swimming boundary now.

"It is a long way," called Isabella.

"Save your breath for swimming. It's getting a bit choppy, isn't it?"

They swam on side by side, lengthening their strokes.

"What do we do when we get there?" she panted.

"Swim back! What do you think?"

"Minx is already there. The cheek! He's climbing up the rope ladder. Let's hope he isn't going to be more trouble."

"Perhaps they'll sail away and take him with them for good."

"I wouldn't say no to that," said Isabella, quite puffed.

They both looked up at the tall side of the boat. A face peered over the side, a friendly face that Isabella knew.

"Hey - Mr Patel," she called. "Mr Patel, it's me, don't you remember? Isabella from the plane!"

"So it is. Hello! Come aboard! Round the other side there's a rope ladder!"

Sam and Isabella swam to the ladder and pulled themselves up, dripping on to the deck.

"How lovely!" said Mr Patel. "But I didn't recognise you without your curls. Ah Tai, have you got a towel for these two, please?"

Isabella and Sam rubbed themselves down.

"That's better," laughed Mr Patel, as Isabella's hair sprang back into curl.

"Now then, Isabella, this is Mr So Man Tai." Mr Patel drew her to his friend.

"And this is Sam, my cousin, same age as me - more or less."

"Call me Ah Tai," said So Man Tai. "Now, what will you have - we're having jasmine tea."

He quickly read that jasmine tea was not exactly what Isabella and Sam had in mind.

"Or we've got orange juice or coke."

"I'll have an orange juice please," she said.

Sam nodded, but he was also watching Isabella. Her eyes were scanning the boat and she had a perplexed look on her face. Then the reason dawned on him. There was a loud crash below. Isabella, catching Sam's eye, rolled hers in dismay.

"Whatever's that?" Both Mr Patel and Ah Tai peered below deck.

"He's everywhere." Isabella looked furious. "I've never seen him like this before."

"Is he downstairs?" whispered Sam.

Mr Patel and his friend went downstairs to investigate.

"Yes, he's been up and down several times - "

"Nothing as far as I can see." Ah Tai was back on deck, followed by Mr Patel.

"Isabella, you and I together seem to put a jinx on things. I think you're psychic," he laughed.

"Well if I am, I'm trying to stamp it out very firmly. I don't want another incident like a storm - tell Sam how bad it was. I don't think he believes me."

"It was bad," said Mr Patel flatly.

"The trouble with you my friend," said Ah Tai, putting his hand on Mr Patel's shoulder, "you're too close to the next world."

"Isabella's interested in all that," continued Mr Patel. "And I told her all about reincarnation and the various gods. Oh - Ah Tai, you can show them some of your carvings. Ah Tai's a stonemason."

Sam, feeling slightly left out, asked, "What does a stonemason do exactly?"

"He makes things in stone," laughed Ah Tai. "I specialise in statues for temples."

"Oh, those scary rude ones," said Isabella.

"Just those - lions and guardian gods for putting outside banks and the homes of important people."

"We went with my sisters the other day to a temple," said Sam, trying to sound very normal, "and I saw a Monkey God, which gave me the creeps."

"Isabella knows all about the Monkey God and how he helped Tripitaka, a wise man, to bring the Buddhist Scriptures from India to China," said her Indian friend.

"But what about Sandy and Pigsy?" Ah Tai opened a solid looking wooden chest. It was full of small stone carvings. "Here we are."

He brought out a small statue of a monster whose hair was painted a flaming red, and it had eyes like lanterns and nine skulls hanging round its neck.

"He's rather sweet - so small - but pretending to be so fierce," smiled Isabella stroking him.

"Oh, but in real life - real life - " Ah Tai laughed at his repetition, "he's very fierce. He ate many men while he was guarding the river - and this, this is Pigsy. He's kinder but helpful too," he said, handing the carving to Sam.

"What about the Monkey God? How does he help?" questioned Sam.

"He's got the brains. You see Tripitaka, well, he's wise and good but he's not always that quick on the uptake. That's where Monkey comes in. He's full of ingenuity. I mean, when he's in trouble, he plucks out his hairs and becomes a thousand monkeys - and you can imagine the havoc that causes."

"Where are the real Sandy and Pigsy now?" asked Isabella.

"In heaven with Tripitaka and the Monkey God," said Mr Patel.

"Then how come they were on earth?" she asked.

"Sandy and Pigsy had always been on earth -

and so had Tripitaka. But they were rewarded for bringing the Scriptures back by being given a place in heaven," said Mr Patel.

"And the Monkey God?" asked Sam.

"He had been banished from heaven by the Jade Emperor. The Monkey God in his poem says:

'Why should heaven's halls have only one master?'

- and so the Jade Emperor banished Monkey from heaven and sent him to help Tripitaka."

"Do you think they could come to earth again?" Isabella was looking intently at Mr Patel.

"Anything could happen with Monkey!" he smiled.

Sam was looking thoughtful but he also could not help noticing that Isabella was looking all over the place, not knowing what to do. Eventually she got up and seemed to be looking over the side of the junk, and at that moment it looked suspiciously to Sam as if she had been given a mighty shove over the side. There was a splash and she returned looking rather pleased with herself.

"I think we'd better be getting back, Bizz. Dad'll be worried," said Sam, downing the last of his orange juice.

"Yes," she agreed. "It's going to take me a bit of time to swim back."

"I hope you'll come and see me at the factory on Lantau Island. It's on the east side. Anyone will tell you." Ah Tai shook hands. "And these are for you," he said, handing Sandy to Isabella and Pigsy to Sam. "You'd better have Sandy, Isabella, to protect you."

"Oh, I couldn't take him," she began.

"Of course you must. Will you be able to carry him while you swim?" he asked.

Isabella looked doubtful.

"Don't worry," said Sam, "if you've got a plastic bag, I can take them both."

They were over the side in a flash, swimming on their backs and waving to Mr Patel and Ah Tai.

"Where's Minx?" asked Sam when they were out of earshot.

"I think he's still on board," began Isabella. "Damn Minx! I don't care where he is. The minute I'd pushed him overboard he was back up again."

"What was he doing?"

"Just being a terrible nuisance. Walking on the table, climbing the mast, balancing on the edge, opening boxes - you name it. Are you okay with the bag?"

"Sure," said Sam who was only using his legs to swim but still finding it quite easy to keep up with his cousin.

"Ow!" squealed Isabella. "He's back. He's really excelling himself today."

Sam and Isabella had got their feet back on the warm sand.

"It's funny we keep hearing that story." Isabella looked at her cousin.

"Yes, it gets to you. But you know what I think - "

"What?"

"I think Ah Tai was aware of Minx," he said.

"You mean he could see him?"

"Maybe. You'd know better than me - could you see Minx all the time? You know, one pair of eyes."

"Honestly, I'm not sure. But shut up, we're nearly there." Isabella smiled at her uncle.

"Sorry! But I knew one of the men on the junk. It was Mr Patel who was with me on the plane."

The pair somehow felt an enormous sense of relief to be back with the family on the beach. The calm sea; distant beach voices; delicious barbecue. But they were tired after their swim and were soon asleep beneath the umbrella and beach towels, cosy in the warmth of their sunburn and soft sea breezes.

"Oh good, you must watch this," said Sam's dad turning on the TV, back at home. "It's a re-run of 'I dream of Genie'. It used to be one of my favourite programmes."

Isabella was curious.

"It's about a man who has a girlfriend that no one can see except himself," said her uncle.

"Oh Dad, do we need that?" Sam looked at his cousin.

"Very snooty! Far too low brow for you, I

suppose," said his mum.

"Do you believe in things like that? Invisible people? Ghosts?" Isabella asked.

"No! Certainly not!" laughed her uncle. "Do you Bizzie-Bo?"

"I'm not sure," she replied, looking round for Minx who was seated before the television engrossed in the show.

That night Sam awoke with a start. He felt a familiar hand on his. Before him was Minx. Sam smiled. Minx, not saying a word, took Sam by the hand to the bedroom door. Sam looked questioningly at his friend, who in response pointed to the statue of Pigsy which was by his bed. Sam thought for a moment. He went to the window and opened the curtains. Above the whirr of the air conditioning, he could hear that a wind was getting up outside. There was a cold and silvery, distant moon occasionally hidden by a dark grey cloud. The weather was changing. Would it be safe to swim back to the junk? For Sam knew that that was what Minx wanted.

For a moment, he pondered going alone with Minx. Then he laughed to himself at the thought of Isabella's indignation. He crept to her room. Molly stirred in her basket and came to lick his hand.

"Go to sleep, Molesey!" he whispered.

He opened Isabella's door. At first he was shocked to find her bed empty.

"What are you doing?" he asked, seeing her kneeling on the chest below the window.

"It's exciting," she said. "The weather's changing. Is there going to be a typhoon?"

"Could be. But listen. I can see Minx." He paused. "He wants me to go back to the junk," said Sam.

"Where is he?" she asked.

"By the door!"

"Hurray!" she whooped quietly. "You've got him back. Does he want me to come too?"

"Of course. Get a towel and put your swimming costume and tracksuit on," he ordered. "I'll see you by the front door. And be quiet!"

Sam thought he must have regained Minx's friendship because he wanted him to return to the junk, something Isabella might not have been prepared to do by herself. It was quite blustery as they cycled downhill to Repulse Bay. Distantly a clock struck two.

"What do you think this is all about?" called Isabella to Sam in front.

"No idea!"

"Do you think we'll have to swim?" Isabella shivered even though the air was hot.

Eerily the cyclist in front of her lit up momentarily, and was then in a ghostly shadow as the moon shone out or was obscured from view. There was something in the elements that was not sleeping tonight.

'And the moon a ghostly galleon,' she thought, comforted by her fondness for the poem.

When they got to the bay they could see the outline of the junk, moving gently as the waves lapped its side. Isabella looked at Sam, admitting only to herself that she felt nervous.

"He's in! Minx is on his way!" said Sam searching Isabella's face.

"Well, what are we waiting for?"

They threw their towels and tracksuits on to the damp sand.

"Not bad!" said Isabella as she plunged into the blackness.

"I always think it feels warmer at night," said Sam.

But as Isabella looked down there was no comforting sand below, just a density containing she knew not what. She tried not to think of sharks. Sam swam just a little behind her.

"Choppy!" he said.

"Is the tide going out?" she asked, turning on her back to look at Sam.

"I think it's just on the turn," said Sam, "going out."

"Is that good?"

"It's all right. I can't feel much of an undertow and we seem to be making headway. Where's Minx?"

"Just here," Isabella said. "Right by me. Can't you see him? He's back with me."

Suddenly a huge wave submerged all three, relentless, white-grey, breaking above their heads. Isabella stifled a sob.

"It's okay, I'm here." Sam was panting by her side.

He could see the look of terror on her face,

terror at the power of the universe and of the unknown which had assumed a new force.

"Sure you want to go on?"

In reply Isabella changed her stroke, onwards with a strong crawl. They were now more than three quarters of the way there.

"Bizzie!" hissed Sam. He didn't dare touch her to attract her attention for fear of making her scream.

"Bizzie!"

Isabella turned on her back reluctantly as she liked to be facing the oncoming breakers.

"There's someone on deck. Swim to the prow! Follow me!"

They went back to breaststroke for the final approach. As the moon reappeared, they saw Ah Tai looking far out to sea. At last they held on to the pointed end of the junk. They bobbed up and down to the roll of the sea.

"Minx!" whispered Isabella. "He's swimming round to the stern. Will Ah Tai see him?"

They both swam a few strokes alongside the boat.

"Oh my goodness!" exclaimed Isabella. "What's happening?"

"What is it? What is it?" panicked Sam.

"It's Minx. He's - lit up. He's shimmering. There's light all around him. He's in full view of Ah Tai lying on his back on a dark patch of sea and he's shining."

They both saw Ah Tai lean over the side of the junk. Suddenly, not only Minx's light but his whole form had disappeared from Isabella's view. The pair pushed off from the side of the junk as it gave a vast judder. Before them was Ah Tai bathed in light, glowing, alive with a new force. Sam and Isabella were spellbound, in awe.

"I can't see Minx," she whispered.

"But Ah Tai can!" Sam was suddenly calmer. How long they remained watching they didn't know. They were lost to this world, out of time and space.

The junk and the sea, the moon and Minx returned as Mr Patel's quiet voice was heard above the sound of the waves.

"I'm on deck," returned Ah Tai's distant voice.

He too was called back. Sam and Isabella swam away in silence, not looking back. The waves crashed above their heads. They were being helped to the shore.

"Let's get back," said Isabella, changing into the comforting warmth of her tracksuit.

It was hard work cycling back up the Peak. A white light, the light of morning, revealed one ghostly scene after another. Minx was helping Isabella from behind. They arrived back to Sam's flat very tired. They sat dazed on a low wall by the pool, looking at the faded lights of the harbour down below, beyond to the airport and further still to Lantau Island.

"I'm shattered," said Isabella quietly.

"And me."

"What do you think happened?" she asked,

her gaze out to sea indicating there was something she felt she'd never fathom.

"Let's not be dramatic," said Sam quietly but firmly. "One thing happened. Ah Tai saw Minx."

"Yes, but is Ah Tai - real?" Isabella was searching for words. "I mean, is he a ghost too?"

"Maybe. But one thing I'm sure of - ghost or not, he's in danger," Sam said the last few words very slowly.

"Danger - from Minx ?"

Sam nodded.

"But why?" asked Isabella.

"Don't ask me to think!" said Sam "It's just what I feel."

"They know each other, don't they?" Isabella continued to look out to sea.

"Yes - " He paused. "I'm going to be busy."

She followed him in silence. No more was said and they closed their bedroom doors with barely a glance at each other. Isabella did not notice that Minx had remained seated on the wall and had continued his indifferent stare out to sea. Their sleep was restless, full of half-formed thoughts and fears.

Chapter 6
A Good Death

Sam and Isabella slept in late.

"Typhoon signal number one's been hoisted," said BeBe grimly, thinking of Joe, the newest, coolest addition to her string of boyfriends.

Isabella looked out of the window. "It's wonderful, wild. Even the harbour's got white horses in it."

"You won't be saying it's wonderful when the building starts to sway," said Sophie. "I hate typhoons. Danger outside and that awful claustrophobic feeling inside with everything shut. You won't like it when the electricity goes off, Bizz."

"Okay then. Let's enjoy it now. Who's for a swim?"

"A swim?" said BeBe. "No fear."

"Well, why not?" said Sophie. "I'll come - provided you mean in the pool."

"And me," said Sam.

There was such a release of tension for Isabella and Sam to be outside in the wind. The air was wild but not menacing. The wind joined in the fun. They were chasing around the pool, diving in, squealing and shrieking. Sam and Sophie raced. He still couldn't beat her. Then there was a diffused flash of lightning and a distant rumble of thunder. It came closer; and then the rain came, huge drops of it, slowly at first, but soon it gathered pace and pelted the surface relentlessly. Sam's mum's voice from a window could just be heard above the watery din.

"You mustn't swim when there's lightning. It's dangerous. Come on! Out!"

And in support of her pleas, a jagged streak lit up the lowering grey of the sky and a crash followed. Squealing even more, they both chased Sophie up three flights of stairs. That's what Isabella called fun.

It was then that she remembered Minx.

"Hey Sam. Have you seen Minx?" she whispered.

"No, not since we were swimming to the junk, I told you."

"And I haven't seen him since we were sitting on the wall last night." Her brow furrowed.

Sam was upset, she could tell.

"I mean what worries you most about his absence?" she queried.

Sam was struggling for words.

Isabella continued, "Well, for me - I'm scared. I don't want Minx around but at least when he is I know what he's doing. I'm going to hate just sitting around in this typhoon. Couldn't we go for a walk or something?"

"Bizz, typhoons are dangerous. Branches come off trees - you know anyway! But I don't think it's going to hit us. Dad said he'd heard on the radio that it was going to turn north. The signal could be down by midnight."

"And Minx?" Isabella pressed.

"I miss Minx - I can't help it. And somehow, I'm not scared, not for myself anyway. Minx, kind of takes me for granted like I do him." Sam looked hard at her. "But I am scared for you and maybe for Ah Tai. I admit Minx is different recently."

"Well that's why you first told me about him, isn't it?"

"Yes, but at that time he was different again - just excessively mischievous, verging on being a nuisance. But he wasn't scary. It's only since you've been on the scene that he's been - well - menacing."

"Oh thanks!" she said. "This is all your fault for dragging me in."

"I suppose it is." Sam looked dejected.

"Oh sorry. I didn't want to make you feel worse. Maybe Minx being a nuisance and all that meant he was going to break out anyway. What makes me laugh is that if you catch his eye, he looks as if butter wouldn't melt in his mouth!"

"I know that look," he smiled, and then added, "but promise me - for the next few days at least, or until he turns up - "

" - if he turns up - " Isabella interjected.

" - if he turns up - we'll stick together. We mustn't get separated. I've been worried about you at night. I could sleep on an air bed with my sleeping bag in your room."

"Your ma would be bound to find out. No, we can't do that. I'll think of something.

Although I've been sleeping so deeply lately that I haven't been scared at night at all."

Typhoon signal number one was taken down at midnight as Sam's dad had predicted and plans were afoot to climb Sunset Peak on Lantau.

"Sam's going to be the only hiker carrying his own weight in food," laughed BeBe.

The six of them set off: Sophie and BeBe plus what their dad referred to as 'their swains', Isabella and Sam. It was cloudy, hot and humid, and the wind was still brisk, but they were in high spirits.

"We must keep to the paths," said Sophie. "You remember last time how we all got split up, going the quick way down - dead straight! It was frightening. BeBe was on one side of a hillside and I was on the other. We were both calling and calling and although we were so close, we couldn't hear each other."

"It was creepy!" BeBe agreed.

Across on the ferry to Silvermine Bay, a short bus ride, and they were in the low foothills. It was a three hour hike to Sunset Peak but worth it, for it was not often in busy Hong Kong that you could get away from it all. They were a motley crew the six of them with their exchange of sunhats. Sophie wore a bush hat in which she thought she looked like Ava Gardner in one of those old movies they show on Sunday afternoons; Alex, her boyfriend in her flowered sunhat; and BeBe in a back to front American baseball cap and a rugby vest that was constantly slipping off her shoulder. Isabella wore a Chinese coolie hat which kept bouncing off her curls, and Sam had a Mao cap he'd borrowed from BeBe's boyfriend Joe. He was hatless, but had his hair tied back with one of BeBe's ribbons. Isabella and Sam exchanged many questioning glances.

Had Minx turned up yet? Was Minx about? Surely Minx wouldn't miss a fun day like this? Could he be following from a distance? What else could he be doing?

They got to the top at one-thirty. The sun had burned off the cloud and they were glad to find a small tree for a shady lunch. Hong Kong Island in the distance, miles of soft blue, balmy air and so quiet.

"Famished!" declared Sam.

And a serious silence ensued whilst the six munched.

"Can we go to the monastery?" asked Isabella.

"Oh yes I'd like to," said Sam.

"You're a weird pair! Just enjoy the view," exclaimed BeBe and when they looked fed up added, "Can't you go on your own?"

"But we won't be able to talk to the monks," said Sam. "Please Soph, just ten minutes. We need you to translate."

"Okay," replied Sophie. "You're always poking into Chinese stuff. You'll turn Chinese one of these days!"

Sam kept quiet, having got the agreement he wanted out of his sister.

"Come on then you two," said Sophie, jumping to her feet. "We'll be back in half an hour."

"I'll come too," said the faithful Alex.

It was only a short way to the Buddhist monastery.

No Minx? Sam's eyes questioned Isabella.

She shook her head. So and so Minx!

The monks were always friendly, always willing to talk - but they spoke Cantonese. They showed them round the bare buildings and displayed their vegetable garden of which they were very proud. Some visitors were in the refectory enjoying a simple vegetarian meal.

"Ask them about their religion," said Sam.

"Well what especially about their religion?" asked Sophie impatiently.

"What they believe in," prompted Isabella. She was not sure what she was expecting.

"Keoi dei sun di mat yer neh?" asked Sophie obediently.

"Saam gao gwai yat," came the reply.

It seemed that their religion was a mixture of Confucianism which amounted to the love of the family. Then there was Taoism which was very mysterious. Isabella loved the Taoist idea of 'The Way', which you had to search for in life and which was always hidden. And then there were the Buddhist Scriptures. Once more Isabella and Sam listened to the story of Tripitaka, the Monkey God, Sandy and Pigsy.

"The Monkey God sounds fun," said Sophie, translating.

The monk gave her a piece of paper, laughing as he did so. It was about the clever, wicked Monkey God.

"I keep hearing about him," said Isabella. "I can't get away from him."

"Soph, do you mind if Bizzie and I go to visit a friend in his factory? It's not too far from here?" asked Sam.

"I'm supposed to be in charge of you - " began Sophie.

"Please Sophie, there are two of us," Isabella added.

"Well, all right. We'll meet you at the club for supper - and whatever happens, Mum says we have to be home by ten if we miss you there," said Sophie in a big sisterly way.

Isabella and Sam set off to find Ah Tai in his stonemason factory. It was just after four when Isabella looked at her watch. They'd been walking slightly down and eastwards for more than half an hour.

"Are you sure this is the way?" she asked.

"It's further than I thought. The old Chinese guy selling ice-cream said you couldn't miss it."

They continued along the narrow path that encircled the hillside for another quarter of an hour.

"I think we're lost, Sam. Shall we give it up? We could always come another time," she suggested.

Sam hated giving up. "Just round the next bend."

They trudged on.

"Got anything left to eat?" he asked.

"A few sandwiches."

"Look! I told you we were on the right path."

Round the bend of the hillside, they came upon a tall concrete building with an enormous yard. It was an ugly gash on the deserted hillside. A wide bumpy track up to it wound out of sight. In the yard there were many large statues and some of them nestled beyond the yard, seemingly at home, in the thick grass, forgotten.

"It looks deserted," said Sam.

"Ah Tai! Ah Tai!" called Isabella.

"Ah Tai!" joined in Sam.

The hillside echoed, "Ah Tai! Ah Tai!"

"Eerie, isn't it?" laughed Isabella nervously.

"Looks as if we've had a wasted journey," said Sam.

He too felt part of another world, but was trying to sound as normal as possible.

"This is just huge." Isabella came close to a a statue about ten feet tall.

"It's the Guardian King of the North." She spoke softly.

"How do you know that?" asked Sam.

"British Museum. He's horrible isn't he?"

"So many hands to reach you. So many skulls. And that poor bod round the back of his head. I wouldn't care to be him." Sam drew back.

"And there's the Monkey God!" said Isabella. "Look at his cap. There's a special place for twisting it tightly at the back of his head when he's naughty. He's quite sweet, don't you think?"

"If you like that sort of thing!" laughed Sam. "Shall we finish the sandwiches? Over here. I don't fancy eating with that lot looking over my shoulder. No sign of Minx, I suppose."

"Oh don't! I'd forgotten all about him - although this is just the kind of place he'd love!" Isabella shivered.

They ate the last of the sandwiches in silence sitting very close to the edge of a precipice, staring out to the distant sea and Hong Kong Island, which looked so friendly and alive. It seemed to emphasise the bleakness of the spot they were in as a thin mist began to swirl around them. The lights grew dimmer. The steep drop filled with mist.

"Is it getting dark already?" Isabella asked, "It's only six-thirty."

"It's the mist. It's just beginning to come down. We'd better get a move on."

"Stay there! I must go to the loo before we set off." Isabella ran to the back of the factory.

The mist was no longer thin. Sam began to cough in response to the thick white coldness.

"Hurry up, Bizz," he called.

Isabella emerged from behind the factory.

"Oh!" she screamed.

She had come bang up against a tall statue. Was it the Guardian King of the North?

The mist had become a thick fog. She was alarmed. The path would not be easy to find.

"Sam! Sam!" she called. There was no reply.

"Sam, cut it out!" She waited. "Sam, where are you? Sa-am!" she screamed loudly now.

The echo was dulled in the white swirling air.

"Sam! Please Sam!"

But there was no reply. She gave a small sob. She was breathing heavily. She could barely see her hand before her. And she was tired - so tired.

"Sam!" she called out again feebly, not expecting a reply.

Then she ran to where she thought her rucksack had been, but drew back. Her stomach turned over as she thought of the terrifying cliff. Backing away, she fell over a small statue. She felt a thin cold hand on hers. All rational thought left her. Only the fear of the unknown and the loneliness of this white world filled her head. The loss of Sam had blanketed any thoughts of action. She wandered around slowly as in a dream, falling, stumbling. She was hurt, but she only distantly felt the pain as if it was part of someone else's body. A wearying fatigue overcame her. She sat down and then slowly stretched herself out on the hard damp ground. She was not cold, but exhausted, empty of feeling, and soon asleep. She was sinking deeper and deeper into an unnatural sleep, defenceless and dead to the world. That cold thin hand was not far away.

Below the mist, in the dense blackness of the night, Sam lay quite still, buried deep in the warmth of the undergrowth. No bat, no bird, no creature stirred about him, as if to shun that cosmic place where that same unnatural sleep had overtaken him. The white hanging mist above him slowly disappeared and he lay open to the stars, a cold moon and the silent music of the night.

The sound that woke him in the red dawn was the movement of his own hand against the bracken. Standing over him, her white garment bathed in the red light, was Kuan Yin, the Goddess of Mercy, guarding him from the terrors of the previous night. He lay locked in her sight until she slowly evaporated into the warm haze of dawn. He had heard Isabella's terrified cries in the mist but he had been held high above the head of the Guardian King of the North. He was petrified, dumb. The Guardian King had transported him down the hillside on his shoulders away from the world into a disembodied sleep.

Sam sat up. A red arc of sun arose above the horizon of sea, lighting a path straight to him. Behind him as he turned to look upwards he saw the figure of Ah Tai on the edge of the precipice. His plain white robe glowed in that same fierce light. And then along to the left, some twenty yards away, Isabella's curls were cascading, red-brown in the morning light, over the cliff. Sam let out a stifled cry, but no sound came as he mouthed her name. He scrambled through the undergrowth that sprang back as he forced his way upwards.

He stood above Isabella, her face and hair

alight in the dawn. She opened her eyes and smiled up at him. Sam took her hand and drew her gently away from that deathly drop. Her face changed into a look of horror.

"Minx!" she cried. She held out her arms in front of her, as if trying to keep Minx at bay.

"Where's Minx?" Sam was trying to calm her.

"Minx!" she cried again. "Oh save him!"

Sam followed Isabella's frightened eyes to the red glow of Ah Tai.

Then Sam too saw his old friend.

Minx had his hand on Ah Tai's shoulder. His friendly gesture only heralded danger and death.

"We must rescue Ah Tai," she said as she moved stealthily forward, Sam in her wake.

But too late. The figure of Ah Tai evaporated into the morning light just as Kuan Yin's had done. Minx stood facing Isabella and held out his hand. She felt herself drawn to him.

"No, no! We must leave this place!" Sam pulled her back.

Minx's spell was broken. Isabella began to run in panic.

Sam steadied her, took her by the shoulders.

"Now let's go calmly," he said, leading her by the hand to the pathway. Isabella constantly turned on her descent to see if Minx was behind them. Right on her heels he followed, never more than a pace away. Down, down to the early morning watery life of the bay. The cousins hurried to the ferry that was just arriving back from Hong Kong Island. A small queue of commuters setting off for work waited. At the kiosk, Sam held out a ten dollar note but his eyes were met by a blank look from the other side of the counter. The pair were forced to move along by a passenger from behind. For a moment they didn't know what to make of this strange behaviour. Then, horribly, suddenly it dawned on Sam that he could see Minx, had seen Minx for the last hour. They could both see Minx together.

"Bizzie. Minx is there right behind you, isn't he?"

Isabella nodded.

"We can both see him," she said.

Her look told Sam she didn't understand this.

"Don't you realise," said Sam. "We're both invisible too. The man in the kiosk couldn't see us. That passenger behind would have walked right through us if we hadn't moved."

She stood stock still.

"Then we're ghosts," she said flatly. "We're ghosts like Minx. He's won. We're part of his world now."

"No! No!" said Sam. "Let's get home. Let's get home to where people know us. We must go to a world that loves us."

They climbed aboard the ferry. It was a long hour. No breeze ruffled their hair. They crossed town. There were few people about when they made their way to the Peak tram. It wheezed and creaked its usual way steeply up the hillside. They ran along the dappled path and down to their block of flats. The front door opened and Sam's dad, on his way to work, came out. Unseen, Sam and Isabella slipped in past him. They longed to stop, to call out to speak to him, but they knew their voices would be unheard. Even Molly failed to greet them. Isabella's bedroom was shut. Opening it quietly they stood in terror, silent before Isabella's sleeping form. Sam led his cousin to his own room and a similar sight, Sam tucked up in bed, was before them.

"It's all right," said Sam. "Go to your room, Bizzie. We're home."

Isabella hesitated for a moment, but Sam was so sure.

"It's all right. Go," he repeated.

He climbed into bed. Isabella left him. As she crossed the sitting room to go to her room, she saw Minx at the big window looking down indifferently at the harbour. She closed her door and once in bed, went into another happier sleep. Of course they had not been missed!

"Come on you two. Up!" Sam's mum had opened both Isabella's and Sam's doors.

"You can't sleep forever!"

Isabella smiled sleepily at the thought.

"It's nearly eleven. You'd better have brunch. We're all out," she called finally, putting her head round Isabella's door. "More than twelve hours in bed! No wonder you two won the tennis!"

Isabella grinned up at her aunt, finding it hard to recollect her thoughts of what had happened on the previous day. She yawned.

"See you later." And Sam's mum was gone.

They had the flat to themselves, or almost.

"Sure you can't see him?" asked Isabella, as Sam appeared in the kitchen.

"Where is he?" he asked.

"By the kitchen door." She looked up angrily at Minx.

"Nope!" said Sam. "And thank goodness for that!"

"I wish we could be alone," she hissed.

"Just ignore him," said Sam. "We've got to carry on the best way we can, avoiding as much danger as possible. I'm not letting you out of my sight."

"Baked beans as well?" she asked.

"You bet. I could eat a horse."

After breakfast they collected their tennis kit together.

"We just need a normal day. There'll be a lot of people at the club. Let's go and swim and have a few sets - " He paused as his eye caught sight of the *South China Morning Post* open on the table by the settee. A small headline read:

'One hit storm leaves one man dead.'

'Typhoon Rose passed several miles to the north of the island at 10.00 p.m. last night. A junk, later discovered to belong to a well-known stonemason and Rotarian from Lantau, was found wrecked to the east of the island early this morning by a fisherman. So Man Tai's (55) body was washed up by the tide. He was believed to have been on board alone. Mr So leaves no relatives in Hong Kong. Foul play is not suspected.'

"Foul play is not suspected. I like that! Bizzie! Look at this!" Sam looked angry, and then sad.

Isabella read quickly murmuring to herself.

"Typhoon Rose - early this morning - " finishing sadly, " - no relatives. Sam! You realise Ah Tai was - was dead when we saw him this morning!"

Sam nodded. "It wasn't a bad storm," he said.

"This is Minx, I'm sure of it," Isabella exploded.

She went to the kitchen door, but Minx in Minx-like fashion stood unconcerned by the big window.

"Foul play is not suspected!" she screamed at him. She turned to Sam. "That hand on Ah Tai's shoulder. But why? What has he got against Ah Tai?"

"He might not have anything against him. He tried to lure you to the edge of the cliff - and as far as I know he's in love with you - wants you as part of his world," said Sam, desperately trying to work it all out.

Isabella shivered involuntarily at his words.

"So why should he want Ah Tai to join him?" she asked.

Sam thought for a moment. "We felt they

knew each other didn't we?"

"Yes - and remember the way Minx behaved on the junk. He was sort of beside himself," she said. "Ah Tai! Who is Ah Tai? No relatives."

"And who is Minx? Minx who's been my friend all these years. He's a ghost - we think - and if he is - why did he come down to earth?"

"Have you got that piece of paper the monk gave us?" asked Isabella.

Sam returned from his bedroom, crumpled paper in hand.

"Oh no! It's in Chinese," he groaned.

Isabella peered over his shoulder. "Turn over," she said, and then he laughed, "What funny English! It's pidgin."

"'Monkey,'" read Sam. "'Monkey very bad boy. Monkey, no father, no mother. Born by magic from earth and sky.'"

Isabella took over in her excitement. "'Monkey come from mountain of fruit and flowers.'" She squinted at the strange handwriting. "'Go through water curtain. Very clever monkey. Now can live forever.'" Isabella couldn't help smiling.

Now Sam read on. "'Monkey always get out of trouble. Plucks at his hairs. Makes one thousand monkeys.' Could that be what I saw in the temple?" Sam's brow furrowed as he looked straight at his cousin.

"'Monkey want go heaven,'" read Isabella. "'Live with Jade Emperor.'"

"Ah, here it is!" cried Sam, and read, "'But

monkey like be boss too, boss more than Jade Emperor. Jade Emperor no like.'"

"I bet he didn't!" interrupted Isabella.

Sam read the last few words. "'And monkey leave Jade Kingdom and go back Earth.' And so monkey was thrown out of heaven for getting above himself, for trying to be the boss!" Sam looked thoughtful.

"And while he was on earth he earned his place back in heaven by helping Tripitaka," said Isabella.

They were both quiet for a moment.

"Do you think the Monkey God could get stroppy in heaven again and get chucked out?" asked Sam.

"Why not?" said Isabella. "That's his character, isn't it? Fun loving, easily bored, ingenious - and it has to be said - vain." Again they were both deep in thought.

Sam caught Isabella's eye. "Are you thinking what I'm thinking?" he spoke in a whisper.

Isabella glanced towards a third person. "I think so."

They both looked as if they had been hit by a thunderbolt.

"I'm scared," admitted Sam.

"Me too!"

"Do you think we should tell somebody?" he asked.

"Don't be stupid, Sam. They'd never believe us. They'd laugh. Put us to bed. Put us away! Oh how could you think of such a thing?" she said scornfully.

"You think Minx is - ?" He stared hard at his cousin.

"Maybe. Maybe all these coincidences of the story of the Scriptures aren't coincidences after all."

"And Ah Tai - he knows Minx - " went on Sam.

"Yes. I think it's possible that just as the Monkey God helped Tripitaka - "

"Tripitaka - Ah Tai - the same person," interrupted Sam.

"Yes - Ah Tai - Tripitaka - same, same. Now Tripitaka came down to help his friend, Monkey."

"But how can we prove this?" he asked.

"I don't think we can," said Isabella, "and I'm not sure we want to."

"No, we're in this deep enough. But what are we going to do about - ?" Sam motioned his head to where he thought Minx was.

Isabella sighed. "Don't ask me. But I'm tired of having a shadow. It's like having athlete's foot. It never goes away."

Sam laughed. "Come on, Bizz. I don't want to think about it any more for the moment. Let's play tennis."

They set out once more that day. It was good to be among the company of lots of people, forced to be normal, unable to talk secretly to each other. But it was just a breather.

Chapter 7
Monkey

"See you in the morning, Bizzie," said Sam rather pointedly to his cousin that evening.

"Not another early night," said Sophie. "You were snoring when we got back last night."

Isabella and Sam exchanged looks.

"I think I'll turn in as well. I think it must be jet lag catching up on me. I'm terribly tired." Isabella got up.

Sam went to his room and made his bed look as if he were in it. Then he took his lilo from the bottom of his wardrobe and found his sleeping bag. The parents had already turned in, so it was only his loving sisters he had to evade. They were supposedly playing Scrabble with Alex and Joe. He opened his bedroom door stealthily and crept across the corridor to Isabella's room. She was already in bed reading.

"Ssh!" Sam put his finger to his lips.

"What on earth are you doing?" Isabella giggled.

"Shut up! What do you think I'm doing?"

"But you can't sleep here. That's ridiculous. I'm okay," she whispered.

"Okay or not, I'm going to pump up the lilo and sleep on the floor over here. You might not be Okay."

"Oh thanks," she replied.

"Well, don't you realise, Bizz, things are

hotting up," he said.

Isabella had to admit this might be true. She was worried but trying to be calm - and she was certainly ignoring Minx's presence totally.

"Where is he?" asked Sam.

"Where he nearly always is," Isabella answered, sounding very irritated. "Looking out of the window and as if butter wouldn't melt in his mouth. The little innocent!"

"Drat! This lilo pump makes a heck of a din," said Sam. "I'll have to blow the stupid thing up."

"You must read this," said Isabella handing him a book as he snuggled into his new bed.

He looked at the title. "'Ghastly Ghosts,' sounds lousy!"

"No, it's brill!" retorted Isabella, "and I should know! And it's mostly got boys in it - so it should suit you."

Half an hour later, Isabella leant over the end of her bed. Sam was sound asleep.

"Some guard!" she muttered and turned out her light, glancing at Minx as she did so. He looked sleepy too, although truth to tell, she'd never' actually caught him asleep. The air conditioning whirred. A silver dollar of a moon shone through the thin curtains. A short time later she heard Sophie and BeBe preparing for bed. In no time at all, the flat was still. And she too fell into a deep and dream-filled sleep.

Minx climbed nimbly, quickly from the chest below the window. He stood for a moment looking at Sam on his lilo bed, as if to influence his friend's sleep. Then quietly he opened the wardrobe door. There was a creak, but his charges did not stir. Minx took out Isabella's white tennis dress and white trainers, her bridal white tennis shoes. Then he picked up her hairbrush. Isabella was lying flat on her stomach. Minx came over to her bed and sat down. Then slowly, gently, with long strokes, he brushed her beautiful curls, arranging them with his thin, cold hand.

He opened wide the bedroom door, then taking Isabella's hand, he helped her to her feet. She was sound asleep. Molly's paws could be heard pattering along the parquet floor. She watched, black and sleek, as Minx placed the bridal gown over Isabella's head. She was ready for their journey. Her tennis shoes made no noise as she and Minx made their way through the moonlit sitting room. Through the front door and they were outside in the soft, welcoming, humid air. Molly climbed back into her basket, circled twice and went back to sleep.

Isabella stared straight ahead as Minx led her by the hand down the narrow path that wound down from the Peak to the town. The foliage was thick and exuded a strong Oriental pungent odour. It was intoxicating and every now and then the moon dappled through the leaves. There were few people on the streets in Central District. It was just before midnight. No trams or buses, but voices wafted from bars, and lights from the expensive shops glared as they displayed their goods.

Minx made for the harbour, but not towards the ferry. Instead he took Isabella many yards from the main crossing to a wallah-wallah which waited for passing late trade. A woman of about forty, wearing a coolie hat on a string round her neck, helped Isabella aboard. The put-put of the engine started. They were bound for Lantau Island, passing through the shadow of a huge liner, now by a fishing boat, just avoiding an oncoming ferry, until the harbour traffic thinned out. A wind blew Isabella's curls as they reached the open channel and were guided by the moonlit path cutting through the waves. They landed away from the harbour to the east and began their stony ascent, their ascent to a small place where Minx had some business. The moon was hidden by the mountain. It was very dark.

Isabella followed Minx, dreamily, obediently. They were climbing and the undergrowth on either side of their stony path was quite tall and thick. On and on they went until the land flattened out into a small plateau. The moon, silver and cold, reappeared. They passed some houses in which there were no lights; no sign of life except for the baying of dogs. Then on the edge of the hamlet, six hungry dogs with curling Chow tails came out of the hillside. They barked, approaching in that purposeful way a pack of dogs has, towards Isabella. Only a few feet away from her, they barked and snarled, some half attacking in a cowardly way from behind, others barring her way. Isabella awoke in fear. Terror gripped her. She saw the dogs, and ran. She ran and ran, Minx at her heels, up, up. She had always been afraid of strange dogs and to be confronted by so many had broken the spell of sleep in which Minx had held her.

Meanwhile, Sam was finding his lilo very wobbly and uncomfortable. He rolled off it on to the hard floor and he too woke with a start. He felt anxious, not immediately knowing why. His thoughts turned to danger; danger for Isabella from Minx. He sat up, and horrified he saw Isabella's duvet was pulled back and there was no sign of her. The bedroom was wide open. Where had she gone? Where had they gone? He left her bedroom closing the door quietly. In his own room he put on his tracksuit and trainers, and went determinedly, not panicking, knowing that he had a life and death job to perform. Molly did not move apart from rolling her eyes upwards to see him as he passed her.

Out in the dank air, hidden amid the thick Peak bushes from prying unsleeping eyes, he looked at his watch. It was one o'clock. How long had they been gone, he wondered? He knew with a sure-fire instinct that they were on Lantau Island, but which part? Had Minx taken Isabella to the monastery? Were they back where he had seen Minx with Ah Tai? But the uncertainty of their exact whereabouts did not dim his resolve. He had begun to run now. Through the bushes he went until he emerged under the light of the moon and the still glaring lights of the town. He made for the Silvermine Bay ferry but it was no longer running. He hurried along the quay. No one took note of his haste until he heard a voice calling,

"Sai yan! Sai yan!" It came from a wallah-wallah.

"You want go Lantau?" she called. "Heoi Lantau?"

Sam ran forwards to her.

"Hai!" he said. "I look - " he touched his eyes as he said this, "I look for - what was the word? - neoi yan." Then he ran his hand through his hair.

"Hak sik ho dor - " He indicated curls. The bits of Cantonese he knew were standing him in good stead alongside his pantomime.

"Tai dor neoi jai sap deem," Sam knew that meant twelve o'clock.

Oh dear, he thought, they were a good hour in front. "Fai dee! Fai dee!" he urged his boat keeper on.

"Hai bindo heio?" he asked.

She indicated that they had gone to the east of the island. This helped Sam. Then they weren't going to the monastery. He racked his brains.

Sam somehow had it in his mind that they were going to a temple. Why was this? He stopped in his tracks - Oh no! Of course, it was

Minx's association with the Monkey God. Somehow Sam hadn't been able to get his head round the idea that Minx and the Monkey God were one. He had pushed it from his mind. Minx! His great friend!

"Think! Think!" he said to himself.

Then his imagination turned to the morning when he and Isabella were coming down from Ah Tai's factory. He had noted that Minx had slipped into a small temple that stood a little way off the track. On and on he ran again. He too heard the dogs bark. They approached him but he was soon away from their territory.

Two miles further on Isabella ran on and up, panting and sobbing. She looked over her shoulder. It was useless. She could never get away from Minx. She threw herself on the ground, her head on her arms. Minx stood above her. She turned, quiet now, to look at him. He seemed sad to see her so distressed. Then he held out his hand. He remained in that position for several minutes. Isabella looked into his sad brown eyes. He offered his hand and she took it. They walked together side by side in the moonlight, calm now.

Away from the road, she noticed a small temple. Minx stopped and looked at it. His face showed an inward struggle but he held firmly to Isabella's hand. Then they strode together through the undergrowth. The main door was locked but Minx led her round to the side, to another low door. He pushed it. It creaked open. They had to duck to get through it. Inside the air was dusty but once her eyes were accustomed to the darkness, Isabella could see the usual stone statues, threatening, rude, like so many she had seen before. Minx hesitated for a moment, but then moved away from her to the Monkey God which stood in the centre of the temple. She leant against one of the other statues, feeling very tired, but she kept her eyes on Minx. Taking very deep breaths as if to puff himself out, Minx went to the back of the Monkey God. Then he placed his hand on Monkey's shoulder. There was a terrible cracking, juddering sound. The ground beneath Isabella shook. The Monkey God was fanning himself, giving her a blurred image of the original statue. The monkey fan shimmered and sparkled, blinding her to Minx's position. This was just as Sam had described his experience at the fortune-teller's temple. The fan was now breaking up and hundreds and hundreds of monkeys had broken away. The din from their chattering was deafening. The door! The door! For a moment she couldn't remember where the door was. She felt as if she couldn't breathe. The air was hot and the dust was rising from the commotion, the commotion of those live, lithe, hairy bodies all about her. She made for where she thought the doorway was. She was coughing and choking from the putrid air. She crashed against a wall. Stunned for a moment, the noise bursting her head, she suddenly saw the square of grey light which indicated the doorway. Through it, out under the cold moonlight, she pushed her way through warm fur and bones. Hand-like claws stroked her head and arms. She screamed, a sound which rent the air and echoed down the hillside to the vigilant ears of Sam.

Isabella ran out into the undergrowth. She could not see Minx. On all sides, brushing against her arms, pressing her from behind, the monkeys led her on. Upwards they pressed, then down again into the valley and up the other side. She ran on, the sound of her sobbing lost amid the din. She dared not stop for fear of the overpowering tumult of primitive life at her heels.

Then the monkeys seemed to be spreading out into a wide semicircle behind and by her sides. And before her, glinting like a huge cascading curtain of jewels, she saw a waterfall many feet wide. By the side of this stood Minx both arms stretched out to greet her.

"No!" she screamed.

But the monkey circle closed in on her. There was no chink through which she could escape. Minx stepped forward proudly to claim her. As his hands touched hers, a great clapping arose from his entourage. He led Isabella through the glistening curtain of water into a huge dark space. It was a cave, deserted long ago. They were alone. It was quiet save for the rush of water. She turned back and could see the moon refracted through the falling water. She felt relief for an instant as she thought she was no longer pursued. Then crashing through that watery wall, hundreds of loping figures emerged blocking out the rays of light. She ran again, panicked into the blackness.

She felt water around her feet, then up to her knees and then her waist. Minx's hand caught hers again leading her deeper into the water. That and the terrible splashing behind her drove her on until involuntarily she found her body moving to a smooth breaststroke. She swam on, now and then feeling Minx's hand on her arm or shoulder. But she could see nothing. The chattering and screaming of the monkeys behind her had given way to the heavy breathing and spluttering of swimming.

And then her head banged against something above her. She raised her hand from the water and felt a rough and slimy ceiling. It was only a few inches, inches of blackness above her head. Her heart was pounding, but she had to go on. She turned on her back, lying flat on the water using only her legs to propel herself along. Every now and then she raised her hand to feel the slime just above her face. She felt her body swoon, give way.

The next thing she knew she was being carried by Minx. Once again she heard the chattering which echoed in the huge cavern. He placed her in a corner where a shaft of light shone. Above her head, many, many feet away, up a narrow shaft, she saw the paling moon. There was another world outside.

And in that world, Sam was rushing up the hillside. He came to the temple and looking inside saw those many statues which had witnessed Isabella's flight. Sam looked around but saw no Monkey God. He guessed what had led up to that awful cry, for he had heard Isabella's scream and then the gruesome chattering. He did not pause to think but headed again up the hillside, down the valley and up the other side, where he had heard those monkey sounds lead. He too came upon the water curtain but no Minx stood sentinel to greet him. And then his trail was dead. The grass by the side of the curtain was trampled. The mud was patterned with hundreds of monkey feet. He climbed up beyond and above the waterfall but saw nothing to make him go on. The chattering had ceased some time ago. Retracing his steps, he stared again at the glinting cascade of water. Stretching his hand out before him, he plunged through the water into the echoing vault beyond. Rays of light behind showed him the extent of the cave. He pressed into the darkness, hearing distantly the last of the splashing monkeys. Sam stopped when he felt the water round his ankles. Dared he go into that inky blackness? But he had to find Isabella. He waded in cautiously but deliberately. Swimming now, like Isabella, he found he had to turn on his back because of the ceiling of rock just above his head. He felt this was madness, but still he went on.

Isabella blinked furiously as the whole cave suddenly lit up with a warm yellow sunlight. Fruit in abundance loaded the tall trees and technicolour flowers were all about her. Minx was standing in the middle of the cave, a crown of white flowers in his hand. The other hand he stretched out towards her.

"No!" she screamed, yet, without knowing why, she moved, compelled towards him. He placed the crown on her dark head, the white flowers mingling with her curls, trailed down her back. The monkey circle clapping and chattering, closed about them. Minx released Isabella's hand and stretched his arms wide to either side of him. The monkeys were instantly silent. The cave resounded with another thunderous noise and Minx was fused with his companions. His body shimmered with a light brighter than the sun. The monkeys were absorbed into him. He and Isabella were alone standing a few yards apart. Minx smiled a slow smile as he loped towards her. He gave a half bound to her side in that clumsy yet agile monkey way. He put his arms about her. She felt the rough hair of his steely arms. She gave a scream which was overtaken by an even more piercing cry of pain from her protector. The sunlight disappeared as quickly as if a light had been turned off. All was blackness save for that shaft of light leading to the open sky. Isabella

DANGEROUS FRIEND

avoiding those hairy arms, fled to that corner.

"Bizzie! Bizzie!" Isabella thought she must be hearing things.

"Sam! Sam!" she sobbed. "Where are you?" She heard his wet trainers on the floor of the cave.

"I'm here in the corner, by the light," she cried again.

"Stay there!" Sam said gently. "I'm just here. It's all right."

He found her and sat down quietly by her side and held her hand. Isabella cried softly with relief. Sam could see the shape of the cave, and slowly Isabella's eyes too became used to the dark again.

"Is he here?" she whispered.

"Minx?"

"Yes. Is he still here?" she said again.

"I don't think so," Sam reassured her.

"Look!" Isabella pointed to a small grey stone object in the middle of the cave. "It's his hat," she said.

"The Monkey God's hat?" asked Sam. "I heard you scream and then there was another terrible cry."

"That was Minx. He became - he became - " She shivered violently. "He turned into a monkey, the Monkey God, wearing that hat."

"But I heard many, many monkeys."

"Yes, they fanned out from the Monkey God in the temple, like you saw - but then Minx took them - to himself - he devoured them."

"Do you think Kuan Yin twisted his hat? Is

that what produced that cry from him?" asked Sam. "She disciplined him?"

"I'm sure of it," she said.

They were both quiet again for some time collecting their thoughts and regaining their strength.

"We've got to go through that water, Bizz," said Sam. "And I don't like it any more than you do."

"We'd better get a move on then," said Isabella, getting to her feet. Her legs felt wobbly. "I've never been so scared," she whispered.

"Are you sure he's not here? You can't see him?" asked Sam.

She shook her head. "I think he's gone for good. Let's not talk about him now. I want to be in broad daylight before we go into that."

They walked to the edge of the water.

"How can we keep together in this blackness?" She gave out a whimper. "I mean, how do we know how wide the stream is? There's a current going across to the right and we could be dragged far away from the entrance to the cave where the waterfall is."

"We've got to risk it. There's only one way back. Swim on your back, Bizz, and we can hold hands." He took her left hand and they entered the water side by side. "Okay. Now turn," he said, exchanging Isabella's left hand for her right. "And remember the pull is to your left now."

Using only their legs they moved smoothly

along close to the surface of the water. Sam kept pace with his cousin. They both, in fear, felt for that low ceiling of rock. After several minutes and many moments of subdued panic, there was hope.

Sam said, "The ceiling's getting higher. Bizzie, give me both your hands."

Isabella trod water and faced Sam.

"Now on your front, breaststroke with your right arm but, please don't leave go of me with your left."

This felt better. They were no longer oppressed by the low ceiling. The air felt fresher.

Isabella pointed. "Is that light? It is! Oh thank God! It's getting lighter!"

"And I can hear the waterfall. Keep going, Bizz. To the light!" said Sam excitedly.

"I can feel the bottom," said Isabella. "Sam, get up!"

They walked through the shallow part of the stream. The waterfall, no longer absorbing the rays of the moon looked dull and grey, but never had a sound, the rush of water, been more welcome to their ears.

"Let's run!" said Isabella. "Let's get away from this place."

Through the water, out into the early morning, they found the path and raced past the temple.

"Horrible place!" she called to Sam.

"Now we'll see!' said Sam.

"See what?" she asked as they approached

the ferry pier.

Sam looked at her. She understood. "Oh, you mean - ?"

"Yes," he said. "At least that dog up the mountain saw us, didn't you think?"

Sam presented his rather sodden ten dollar note.

"Jo san," said the man in the kiosk.

"Jo san!" Sam grinned, looking over his shoulder at Isabella.

On the ferry, Isabella threw her crown of white flowers into the sea. It floated, lilies on the water, and then was swept out into the ocean. They both slept. Then it was a dash through Central District with a bag of Chinese sour plums, Isabella's favourite snack. Never had they tasted so delicious. By the time they reached Sam's block of flats the sun was truly up and the heat of the day had begun in earnest. They sat on the wall overlooking the harbour. Even at six in the morning, the hum of Hong Kong life reached their ears.

Sam listened to the horrors of Isabella's night and filled in his exploits.

"You know that was really brave, Sam, swimming in that stream - that slimy roof - "

"Well, you did it!"

"Yes, but I had to - anyway thanks." She stood on her tiptoes and kissed his cheek.

"Hey - cut it out, Bizz. None of that stuff!" he laughed. "Look there's the postman - wave - !"

They both waved furiously and - oh relief -

he waved back. They were still alive!

"It wasn't bad being dead, though, was it?" said Isabella.

"I don't think we were dead - just between worlds - like Minx. But do you think Ah Tai really was Tripitaka?" he asked.

Isabella thought for an instant.

"From the moment you told me about Minx, Tripitaka and the Monkey God kept cropping up. Yes, I'm sure he was. I think Minx got stroppy - up there - " she said, pointing to the rosy sky above, " - he got pushed out of heaven - and Ah Tai - Tripitaka - came down to look for him, just as he'd been helped centuries ago by the Monkey God."

"But do you really believe in all that stuff?" Sam smiled.

"Of course. We have to! But I doubt if we'll convince anyone else. Do you think they're back with the Jade Emperor and that Minx is in a whole load of trouble?" she giggled.

"Search me!" laughed Sam.

"But there is one question," challenged Isabella. "Why do you think Minx, the Monkey God, chose you to latch on to?"

Sam looked into the middle distance. "Obvious," he said.

Isabella waited.

"It's because I'm good, kind, - er - Chinese-loving - how do the French say it - ? Sympathique - !"

Isabella gave him an almighty shove which

almost knocked him off the wall.

"Hey - Bizz!"

"Okay then Mr Wonderful, I'm ready for tennis. Best of three sets. Then we'll see who's really best!" she laughed. "I'm ready any time. Let's leave a note for Mum and get our racquets right now - and then breakfast at the club."

They dashed upstairs.

"I'm having egg and bacon." Isabella's voice floated through the thick bushes as they tramped their way back down from the Peak once more.

"And baked beans, two fried eggs - oh - and sausages," added Sam.

The imagined delights of their breakfast wafted up the hillside even overcoming the smells of a Hong Kong morning.

DANGEROUS FRIEND